Shared Between Them

Korey Mae Johnson

Copyright © 2013 Korey Mae Johnson and Stormy Night Publications

www.stormynightpublications.com

Cover designed by Korey Mae Johnson
www.koreymaejohnson.com

Image Credits:
Images by Bigstock/Andrushko Galyna and The Killion Group

All rights reserved.
1st Edition. February 2013

ISBN-13: 978-1490477374
ISBN-10: 1490477373

All names, characters and events featured in this novel are imaginary. They are not inspired by any individual person, or incidents or events by any individual person or by incidents or events known or unknown to the author. Any resemblance to persons, living or dead, is purely coincidental.

FOR 18+ AUDIENCE ONLY

This book is intended for adults only. Spanking and other sexual activities represented in this book are fantasies only, intended for adults. Nothing in this book should be interpreted as Stormy Night Publication's or the author's advocating any non-consensual spanking activity or the spanking of minors.

CHAPTER ONE

Taric looked around at the dark, shrouded forest surrounding him, the terrain shadowy with mossy greens and blues. It was high noon, and the forest still seemed dark and foreboding all around them. He had been forced to dismount his horse because of all the low branches, and the horse repeatedly neighed its distaste for the place, snorting and stomping around Taric's feet. The creature was unsettled too.

"You know how people say this forest is haunted?" Taric's cousin Draevan asked, as he sliced his and his horse's way through another set of thick cobwebs that hung over the branches like gluey drapery.

Taric was already rolling his eyes at the comment. Taric's aunt, Draevan's mother, had been a seer. He could, and did, believe in some people with supernatural abilities, but he simply wasn't going to buy into every single myth out there, especially those that pertained to ghosts.

"I'm just saying," Draevan said, reading into the doubt Taric was presently radiating about his person, "that it feels like we're being watched."

"You've been saying that for three days," Taric reminded, hacking his sword through overgrowth on the trail. It looked as if no one had walked through this section of the woods for years. The nearest village was about a four-day walk through landscape that was less than hospitable.

"Because it's felt like someone's been watching us since three days ago," Draevan clarified with a grumble. Draevan raked his hands through his shaggy blonde hair as if he were worried that a spider had landed in it. He frowned and continued, "Where is this giant, anyway? For all the babble we heard about death for any who step into the Blue Forest, we've yet to see that goddamned thing, and we've taken more than a step or two! I haven't even seen a footprint."

"We'll find the giant, Draevan," Taric assured with a laugh in his tone. He was certain that he and Draevan were the only people in the world who would want to cross the giant's path… And even that was only because his aunt had foretold that they'd be the ones who'd finally defeat it. "Don't you worry."

"I'm not worrying," Draevan assured tersely. "I'm just saying that the sooner we do this, the sooner we're done with this."

"Very profound," Taric teased with a grunt.

"Fuck off. You know what I mean." He turned around, a grin on his face that foretold clearly that he was about to talk about some tavern wench's posterior. "So, did you see the ass on Amelia?"

"Amelia…" Taric hummed thoughtfully.

"It was that wench at the alehouse four days ago. The one that does that little dance…" He stopped talking to jump over a short ravine. He growled with satisfaction at the memory. "The only thing better than that dance was the one she was doing in the bedroom with me afterwards. The woman could suck a cock like no one's business too."

A giggle suddenly lit through the canopy overhead. They whipped their heads up, instantly stopping in their tracks, but when they looked in the direction of the giggle, which had certainly come from a female, there was nothing there.

Taric and Draevan exchanged uncanny glances until Draevan waved towards the canopy overhead and said, "See?" as if that proved anything.

"Was probably the wind," Taric replied, shrugging his shoulders and walking farther into the forest.

"Wind, my ass!" Draevan snapped, stomping quickly along to catch up with him. "Just admit that something strange is going on. First, there was that flute playing at all hours of the night—"

Taric waved his hand as if he could physically brush this days-old argument away. "Well, *that* was definitely the wind."

"Taric, it had a *chorus*. Wind doesn't often howl in a structured manner."

He was very decided about this, Taric realized, and Draevan wasn't a man who would change his mind about anything once it was made.

"Fine, fine," Taric said, just to let the subject go. "It was ghosts. Now what do you want us to do about it?"

"Nothing," Draevan admitted in his low, gruff tone, kicking a shrub in front of his boot. "I just wanted it acknowledged, that's all. Nothing you can do about ghosts. Not that I know of, anyway. Still leads me to wonder, though, why the hell they'd decide to be annoying."

"Well, that's just not very nice!" a girl's voice suddenly huffed from the trees overhead. "Besides, how is it that I'm annoying *you*? You're in *my* woods."

Taric swore under his breath, the clarity of the voice becoming less and less supernatural-sounding as it came closer. "It's an elf," he realized. He had never seen an elf before, but he did know their hidden kingdom couldn't be too far away. It was rumored to be somewhere beyond the Crystal Mountains, and though they were in that region, they'd never seen anything that made it seem like civilization was near at hand, nor had they ever met a human man who claimed to know how to get there. Elves dealt with dwarves far more than they'd ever dealt with humans.

"Show yourself!" Draevan snapped firmly, drawling out his sword, though he surly knew it wouldn't do him any good. As much as elves reportedly loved watching executions, they didn't murder, and they didn't fight wars. Instead, they were good at hiding and even better at running away. It was said that elves could become entirely invisible if they wanted to... But they were normally much more silent than this one was being. He could hear footfalls crackle upon dead leaves as the creature walked near.

"Ask nicely," the voice reproved teasingly.

Draevan's face contorted. It couldn't be more obvious that he didn't want to play games.

"I'm waiting!" the voice chimed. It was hard to tell exactly what direction the voice was coming from. Sometimes it seemed like it was coming from the west, at other times the south...

"Show yourself *now*, Elf," Draevan demanded in a low growl.

There was a whistle behind them, and they spun to see... a *girl* sitting up on a tree branch, her face merry, seeming like a child on a swing. But she was no child.

She was a beautiful elf-maiden like they'd never imagined. He'd heard that all elves had tattoos all over their bodies, even on their eyelids, and piercings throughout their face, ears, and noses. He'd also heard that elves had red smiles because of all the bitter, red fruit they ate which stained their teeth.

This girl had eyes as large as silver coins, a button nose, and was smiling with a row of straight, white teeth. Her skin was unmarred and pale, and her fingernails looked like they were made of glass. Her long, ivory hair was braided intricately to seemingly accentuate the points on her ear tips, but the bulk of her long braid was draped over her shoulder like a white, shimmery rope. She peered at them with eyes as gold as thick honey.

"Would it have killed you to ask me nicely? You are guests in *my home*, after all," she said, then bit her lip thoughtfully. After a second, she added, "Well, until the giant eats you, that is."

Taric put his sword away, feeling quite disarmed even with it out. Draevan looked lost as he regarded the girl, as if he had wanted a fight but got something he could have never anticipated instead. His shoulders were sagging, and his eyebrows were crunched. "Have you been following us this whole time?"

"No," the girl made a snorting laugh sound with her nose. She kicked her legs playfully in the air under her branch. "Just for the last three days or so."

Draevan hummed and lifted his eyebrows at Taric in an obvious I-told-you-so gesture.

Taric did his best to ignore him. He hated being wrong. "And why?"

"Taric, isn't it?" she said, pointing her finger to him. "And Draevan," she pointed to his cousin, whose shoulders straightened in response. She grinned, "Well, I followed you for a few days because it's my home, and therefore, what you do here is my business, savvy? I thought people were well-done with trying to have a go with the giant. It never works out." She stopped kicking her legs, a serious look finally settling on her face. "And I do mean *never*, Northlanders. That giant has been out there for nine hundred years. Do you know how many times he's been killed? Here's a hint: he's still around to *tell you*."

Taric couldn't help but grin at her concern, even if his grin made her look at him like he was nuts. A little wrinkle formed between her dark eyebrows. It was somehow extremely endearing. "You're a cute little thing," he observed. He had never wanted to just pick up a girl and squeeze her before, but he was becoming overcome with the desire to do just that.

Her face pouted for a moment as if he'd just compared her to a forest critter. "And you're a dumb big thing," she assured firmly. "If you start heading that way now," she said, pointing behind them, "you might be able to save your skins. *Maybe.*" She grimaced as if their prospects weren't very good. "You know the giant's cave is only another twenty miles from here, right down that path." The direction she was pointing bore no path whatsoever. It was even more grown-over than the terrain they were trying to trail-blaze. The undergrowth was only just low enough to walk through.

Draevan made a sound that Taric had never heard him make before. It was an amused sort of grunt that was almost *flirtatious*... And Draevan wasn't a flirtatious man. He was the sort that was perfectly happy to pay for what he wanted and then take it hard. In all his life, Taric had never even seen the man smile at a woman kindly. "Twenty miles is quite far in this," he reminded skeptically. He smiled boyishly at the little elfling, making Taric think he was acting even stranger, but she didn't return the grin.

She shook her head as she differed, "Not when you're a giant." She glanced towards the horse's saddle bags with a glint in her eye.

Suddenly, Taric had a bad feeling about her. It was odd for him to have them—Draevan normally had a no-fail sense about people. He used to have a nearly uncanny ability to spot traitors or anyone who meant to do him or Taric any ill. Their grandfather used to swear by it.

He didn't make an accusation, however, because the elf maiden came right out and said, "Well, I'm not going to argue with you. I suppose humans are cute in the way you tramp all this way, and go through all this trouble, just to get eaten. Besides, I haven't had a payday in far too long."

"*She plans to rob us,*" Taric rumbled in a secret language, one he and Draevan had been developing since they were small boys on stick horses.

"*Aye,*" Draevan agreed, his expression not changing.

He continued to look up at her with amusement. "*She does. Can't be a very successful thief, though. She's wearing a dead man's boots and a dead man's coat... She's a scavenger.*"

Taric was so busy being entranced by her angelic little face that he hadn't looked at the rest of her body. Draevan was right. The clothes she wore were very old, very dirty, and far too large for her. She probably waited for men to come looking to kill the giant and then plucked as many earthly goods from those warriors as possible as they searched through the woods.

"There's that stupid language again!" she grumbled unhappily. "What sort of language is that?" she demanded, looking very annoyed. It was proof enough that she had been keeping them company for at least a while. He and Draevan hadn't bothered to speak in their secret tongue all day.

"If you've come to steal from us, elfling," Taric told her, ignoring her question. He straightened, trying to make himself seem even larger, hoping to intimidate her into behaving. "I'd warn you away from that. We know how to teach a lady not to play with fire."

Her eyes widened in surprise, but she recovered her reaction until she was looking out at him through slits between her long, black eyelashes. "No, no. *You* are the ones playing with fire. I consider you both as good as corpses, and you can't take your wealth with you."

Taric gave a singular laugh at being called wealthy. Perhaps in comparison to her they seemed well-to-do, but they were far from considering themselves rich-men. That's something they hoped to remedy on this adventure—that, and their marriage.

Long ago, the king of the elves decreed that whoever would slay the giant and bring back a golden shield that the kingdom had lost nearly a millennia ago that the giant now kept on his person, would be given an elf-maiden of the victor's choice as payment for the service.

Draevan and Taric found themselves, in that case,

between two prophecies told in the North: that the slayer of the Dark Wizard, the scourge of half the world and enemy to the Western Realm, would be killed by the spawn of an elf and a giant-slayer. And Draevan and Taric, when they were boys, were foretold to be the slayers of that giant. In short—the Dark Wizard's time was drawing near... As long as something wasn't misunderstood.

"Don't you worry about us, pet," Draevan scolded, though a smirk still hadn't disappeared from his face. "Just worry about yourself. We don't take kindly to thieves, but I tell you what: you keep your hands to yourself, and we'll keep *our* hands to *our*selves."

She frowned. "You're not as fun as I thought you'd be," she openly pouted like a little girl who couldn't get anyone to join her for a tea party. She contorted her body and pulled herself up until the feet of her boots perched on the branch she'd been sitting upon. "I come out to warn you, and I get threats and accusations in kind!" She slipped off the branch, stomped behind the dark, ominous oak she had been seated on, and promptly disappeared.

The men just stood silent and looked at the tree. Eventually, they walked around it, looking up at the climbing branches, but saw no trace of the elf. "*Well, she's still around, I guarantee it,*" Draevan grumbled.

Taric agreed. "*And she'll be back to rob us blind before tomorrow when we meet this giant,*" he ascertained. "*This is her window of opportunity.*"

Draevan turned and raised an eyebrow. Normally, thieves would make him bunch up his fists and scream swears to the world around them. This time, however, Draevan was rolling his shoulders back with excitement. "*Well, let's get ourselves ready for her visit then, shall we, Cousin?*" he asked him mischievously.

Taric stifled a laugh, realizing instantly what Draevan planned—to set a little trap. Tonight was going to be very interesting, indeed. "*Well,*" Taric replied. "*It'll surely get us used to the feel of an elf-wife.*" He pointed to Draevan then and reminded, "But I was right about there not being ghosts."

Draevan smiled with his whole face. "I've never been so happy about your being right."

* * *

Finally! The humans were asleep. It was nearly sad, as Kyra watched them drink the afternoon away while laughing and joking with each other, knowing that it was their last night with such joys. They'd surely die tomorrow, fast if they were lucky, very slowly and painfully if they got the giant in too bad of a mood first. She guessed on the latter. There was something hardened about these men that Kyra couldn't help but recognize. They'd surely succeed in using their weapons on the giant, but that would only piss him off.

It still bothered her that she couldn't put her finger on the language they would sometimes speak in. Their accents were known to her: they were from the Northern villages, beyond the Crystal Mountains… But she still didn't understand their tongue, and until now she had been quite confident in thinking that she'd heard all the northern languages before. Apparently, she had been wrong.

She stifled a sigh, trying to be as silent as possible, but she couldn't help but think of her brothers, three of whom had raised her but were now very dead: one by the giant and the other two by the hangman's noose in the middle of the elven kingdom. Any one of them would have been able to understand the language spoken by these two human men; they had been so smart and clever… before they were hunted down like dogs.

The human men had unsaddled their horses to give the beasts rest, and unfortunately they were using the saddles as pillows. This was not uncommon, but it always made getting her loot more difficult; most men kept their gold coins in a bag they tied to their saddle. Even worse was when they hid their coin in their boots—like she did. She'd taken the boots off a corpse once, and although they were too big for her, she fell in love with the hollowed-out sole that allowed her to keep her coins, and even a spare weapon or two, safely hidden beneath her feet.

She bit her lip and slowly approached the men's camp, where they had hunkered down in knee-high grass, using the carpet of the forest and a couple of bedrolls as a mattress. A small fire burned by their feet, though it wasn't even nightfall yet. Even with the fire, she realized it would be better to try to make her move now, before it became too dark to see. Humans always had the advantage when it came to total darkness, since elves' eyes weren't as sharp. Elves were much weaker in body, and they probably would have been killed off years ago if they hadn't had some magical ability.

The hulking Draevan gave a loud snore just as she was reaching out to his saddle. The sudden sound nearly made her jump backwards. Wearily, she took a relaxing breath and bent down closer to Draevan's saddle, pulling coins out of a purse secured around the horn. She smirked and then turned towards the other one.

There was a sudden tightening around her ankle. She paused. All she was able to do was mutter "Damn!" wearily, just before a rope yanked her violently from the ground and then up a tree, until she found herself swaying back and forth and upside down by a thick, low-hanging oak branch.

She recognized the full indignity of being caught in the same manner as one might catch a rabbit and was suitably furious. "Son of a bitch!" she cried, then looked at the upside down image of the two men climbing easily to their feet.

They didn't even look drunk now! They had stumbled to their make-shift beds not thirty minutes before… This didn't make any sense.

She had been tricked! And they added insult to injury when Draevan crowed with laughter. "Eenie, meanie, minie, moe. Catch a she-elf by her toe…"

"Get me down!" she cried, realizing that she had let herself go back to her visible state during the shock of being captured. She pulled her shirt down—or up, rather—over her belly-button, since it seemed to want to expose her breasts with the help of gravity. "Put me down right now!" She tried to bend in a way that would free the rope lasso from around her boot, but she didn't even come close to completing the maneuver before her muscles trembled from the strain and then straightened with defeat. She let herself hang and sway, grumbling. "When did you even find time to do this? I was watching you all afternoon!" she cried.

"You were watching us, but not carefully enough. We've done this before. Enemies are easily distracted," said Taric as he brushed his black hair back out of his eyes. "Got any weapons on you?" he asked.

"No," she lied, pressing her lips together stubbornly.

She was searched anyway. Draevan came up to her and patted his ridiculously large hands up and down her squirming body. "Ogre," she grumbled as he found a slingshot in her pocket and a dagger strapped to her upper arm.

"You are quite a different sort of elf," Taric grumbled. His tone sounded like he was trying to be angry but still only coming up as amused. He must have been referring to elves not being creatures known to carry weapons… And he would have been right if he hadn't been talking to the last descendant of a long, tragic line of outcasts. Her family had to make-do to survive.

"The only thing I hate worse than violence," she defended tersely in defense, "is when it's being done to *me*!"

He pulled her coat completely off of her, and yet another knife hit the ground. "Careful!" she snapped. "You're gonna cut me that way!"

"You could have told us the truth, dove," Draevan

replied firmly. "No weapons, indeed! If I find one more—just *one more*—I'm stripping you naked. Even an idiot knows to throw down his arms when he has no other choice."

"Well, I'm a special kind of idiot," she replied, although his threat was alarming enough. She wasn't about to come clean about what was hidden in her boots; she was hoping for the best, and they were her last defense. Without weapons, she wouldn't have a prayer in fighting either of these two behemoths off. They were massive, hard-bodied men.

He gave a wry laugh. "I guess so." Even though she struggled, he had no problem binding her hands together with a piece of leather. He looked at Taric and said, "Cut her down. We need to get her boots off. If they're a dead man's, she's probably using them for storage."

Her brow ruffled. "How'd you know they're not *my* boots?" she asked, quite astonished.

"Your foot ends about here." He squeezed her toe, which ended halfway through her boot. "Don't you know it's unlucky to wear a dead man's boots?"

She pursed her lips, but was quickly feeling unease as blood continued to rush to her face. She wondered how much longer it would be before her face turned purple. "That would explain a lot…"

Draevan scooped his massive arm around her body, and when Taric cut the rope tied to her feet, he neatly adjusted her body so that she was cradled in his arms. She looked down at the ground beneath her. Damn, he was tall… She had never been this close to either of them and hadn't really considered how tall they'd be up close. He would have dwarfed even her brothers in comparison.

She kicked her feet, struggling to get out of his grasp, but Taric jumped forward to aid him and pulled her boots off. They came off easily, being so large for her, and he quickly upheld one, pulled out the inside sole, and several knives, coins, and small trinkets fell out. They had apparently run into those sorts of boots long before they met her, and often enough that it was apparently something they expected from a thief.

Still, Taric looked at her and lifted an eyebrow, silently accusing her of, once again, lying about not being armed.

"Alright, so you caught me," she growled. "I don't have a pot of gold or anything, so I fail to see what you gain by this."

"What's *not* to be gained by this?" Draevan replied curtly, dropping her bare feet onto the grass. She tried to run, but got stopped mid-step as Draevan grabbed at her tunic.

Her eyes went wide. "No!" she growled as she fought against him. With a loud tearing noise, Draevan had ripped her shirt into two pieces at the seam. "Stop!"

He didn't; he merely continued to tear the rest of the fabric completely from her bound arms and threw it onto the ground in tatters.

She shot a terrified glance towards the leaner, and seemingly more cultured, Taric. "Please," she begged him.

She immediately lost hope in gaining his assistance when she saw that his eyes weren't on hers. They were looking at her bare, exposed breasts. She wanted to get swallowed up by the earth and die; never before had her breasts been seen by a male. Her throat tightened, a cry getting stuck in her throat, unable to contemplate her current modification or fear.

Massive arms reached around her from behind and unlatched the clasp at her belt. Her pants, pulled from a body far larger than her own, fell off her hips and right onto the ground around her. Her thin underwear came down moments after that, and she sunk down low, bending herself in a way that she hoped would hide some of her nudity.

Taric merely gazed hungrily at her with those icy-blue eyes of his, a curt smile curling at his lips. She looked at his boots to avoid the leering gaze.

"*Now,*" Taric said as Draevan came along beside her, leering down at all of her skin and holding her by her elbow, "I think she's unarmed."

"You can't treat me like this!" she gasped, feeling out of breath from the shock of her miserable situation and her treatment. She knew she wasn't attractive enough for them to be actually aroused, thank the gods, but the humiliation stabbed at her like a blade in her heart. "What have I done to you?" She meant to raise his eyes and pierce him with a hurt look, but she couldn't do it. In fact, she squinted her eyes shut so she wouldn't have to look at anything at all.

"You tried to steal from us, for one. And I warned you to come clean about the weapons, didn't I?" lectured Draevan pedantically.

She began to shiver violently from the cold on her skin and curled her toes into the cold, moist ground under her feet, unable to find warmth. Noticing her misery, Draevan grumbled and swooped her up into his arms.

She took a deep breath, surprised by the way her body clung comfortably to the heat he emitted. At least she wasn't knee-deep in cold grass any longer. Draevan shifted her weight in his arms and said to Taric, "I say we fuck the daylights out of her. She's a ripe little thing." She felt a wave of nausea when he said this, but upon his expression, she found herself relaxing. There was only mischief in Draevan's eyes, and far too much of it for his words to be believed. "Besides, it's never been done before—a human-elf coupling. I say we practice up for when we claim our elf-bride."

Taric smirked. "Why would we *reward her* for trying to rob us blind?" he replied, squaring his shoulders suavely. He looked at her as if to say, 'What do you have to say for yourself, young lady?'

She didn't answer that look. "Robbing is a dark way to look at this little visit!" she defended sharply, after he glared in her direction long enough. "Besides, I'm not the one manhandling a harmless female!"

She sniffed the air indignantly, and was surprised. Draevan smelt surprisingly good; not like food, but strangely like the rain after a storm—earthy, yet fresh.

She squirmed to get more comfortable, adding, "I like to think of this like I was a neighbor, simply borrowing a cup of sugar from some friendly-looking folks. One that I don't plan to return since you'll both be dead by tomorrow evening. Don't forget that—you being dead in the morning is very important to looking at this situation the proper way. Anyway, I don't know what it's like in the Northern Lands, but around here we don't strip people who come about borrowing things!"

Taric continued to look at her like she should be ashamed of herself. She sighed with resignation. "Fine," she huffed. "I was a very naughty girl. Is that what you want me to say? I still don't deserve this treatment!"

"You're a thief! Do you *feel* shame?" Taric asked her, looking both amused and exasperated, which was a mixture of emotion she'd only seen on her brothers.

"Let me think…" she replied, looking up at the tree canopy above. "No! You're the ones that should be shamed! Me, on the other hand… I can't afford shame. I'm too poor."

"Well, I think we can spare you some," Draevan replied, stepping backwards towards a log resting on the ground nearby. "Consider this helping of shame *on the house*, our death not even required in this transaction!" He sat down on the old, hallowed log and flipped her body over his lap as if she were merely an oversized pancake. She kicked her bare feet, but she only stubbed her toe for all her trouble.

She had no idea what he was doing, and her attention was too wrapped up in her hurting toe, before Draevan's rough, overly large hand smacked down heavily on her bare bottom.

"Nyah!" she squeaked, aghast. "You can't—" She

stopped the sentence there. She couldn't even mouth the word, '*spank*'. It would have been embarrassing enough if she was a four-year-old child heading over her father's knee for some discipline.

But she didn't have one of those fathers. In fact, she had no parents at all that she could remember. Her brothers were her world since she was a babe, and they were... well, they weren't disciplinarians. They were jesters and jokers and thieves. Lying, stealing, or cheating and getting away with it was rewarded, not repressed.

Strangely, the embarrassment wasn't the worst part, although humiliation here was in no small measure. The most awful part was certainly the pain produced by the punishing palm that came down on her flesh again and again, echoing the sounds of her punishment through the trees. "You're being ridiculous! Stop it! Stop it!"

Draevan's hand had the ability to nearly cover the entire span of her flesh. Now that it was in pain, her bottom felt so sensitive that she believed she could feel his hand even when it only hovered over her skin.

"Let me know if you need me to take off my belt, Draevan," Taric said encouragingly to Draevan over the noise of her growling and angry chirps. She felt a surge of hate fly through her body.

"Go fuck yourselves, both of you!" she hissed, unable to imagine this torture getting any worse.

There was a whistle above her head. "Hear that sort of language coming out of such a pretty little thing? Damn shame," Draevan said reproachfully. "On second thought, that belt might come in handy, Cousin."

"Coming right up." She heard the horrible sound of his belt whooshing through his trousers' loops. While she was following them for the last three days, she had decided that Draevan was the brutish one and that Taric was more the soft and intellectual type, mostly because Taric was more skeptical by far and had a leaner, yet taller, build than Draevan had.

Still, even though Taric wasn't the one punishing her directly, she hated them equally.

She felt Draevan's body shift as he reached for the belt. She couldn't do much to protect her bottom because of how her hands were tied to the small of her back, but she found herself willing to stretch herself backwards as much as she could to try to make covering the tender flesh back there possible. Draevan simply shoved her back down, so she responded by bucking on his lap like a mad horse. "Don't. You. Dare!" He dared indeed, because the belt slapped down firmly across both of her cheeks, leaving a white stripe of pain in its wake. "Fuck!" she cried angrily.

She felt her status as an elf rapidly declining. It was unheard of for one of her people to be in such a position—stripped, bare-assed, and unwed, over a human man's knee. She forced herself as best she could not to think about how much of her most private anatomy they could see, which was surely more than she'd seen of herself.

"Genuine elf-bottom," Draevan said approvingly, ignoring her agitation. "Good thing we'll be given one of these soon enough! Hopefully we'd get to see *her* in this position as well." Just as she was busy not appreciating how casual he was about spanking her, Draevan brought the belt down again with a loud CRACK! that was so loud, she felt her heart skip a beat from the shock.

"Ouch!" she cried. Damn it all, that *hurt*! Why would anyone even spank a child this way? It was torture! She felt she was losing her composure—fast. Her heart began to race as the stinging pain increased with every slap. "Okay, you've had your fun. Stop! Stop now!" Each word she spoke betrayed her agony and desperation. "Stop it! Stop it, please!"

She was more than certain that she was the first elf in history to have said 'please' to a human. She was exploring all sorts of taboo behavior today! She was nearly thankful her brothers were dead; if they knew about this, they'd never let her live it down.

"All joking aside, little elf, you've earned yourself a good solid hiding. Now be a good girl and take your medicine," Draevan replied unsympathetically, somehow even firming his grip on her, making it so she could barely buck or squirm around on his lap.

That was probably for the best since her kicks and squirms, it came to mind, probably made her look like she was a naughty three-year-old being taken in hand. "I'm nineteen years old! You can't do this!" she tried, openly frustrated by all this.

By now, it felt like a million fire-ants were biting her.

"Oh, come now. A woman's never too old for a well-needed spanking," Taric replied above her. "Drae, you missed a spot."

"I hate you! I hate you both! I can't wait until you're eaten, *and you will be*!" She was quickly beginning to wish that the giant wasn't deaf, because her cries would lead the creature right to these men.

"Nnnooo!" she cried. Then, at last, she felt the leather bindings slipping away. Her hands were free! She grasped at Draevan's leg, trying to heave herself off, but he wasn't having any of her escape attempts, and held her tighter, pressing her chest to his thigh.

"No need to be so angry at us just because you're a bad thief," Draevan clucked. "Taric, can you hold her hands down? She's getting a little dramatic, and I'm not near done," he asked Taric with the sort of casualness that was reserved for ordering a beer at a tavern.

"Okay, okay!" she cried, as if she had completely succumb to this inquisition.

Only it wasn't an inquisition, so even though she actually said, "I'm sorry! Is that what you want? An apology?" it didn't help her a jot.

"I want you to stop making a racket, so we can teach you not to steal without our ears bleeding." Draevan didn't sound very sympathetic at all, which meant Taric wouldn't be, either. After all, only Draevan knew how hard he was hitting her.

He stopped spanking only long enough to adjust her on his lap so she wasn't half-way falling onto the ground like she was now. Lord, it hurt still even though he wasn't currently smacking her! Her skin burned heatedly and stung, and she wanted so much just to reach back and rub the pain away...

SMACK. And the pain returned. Somehow, thinking for a moment that it might be all over after all and then it not being over was too much to bear. Her lip trembled as she felt her eyes begin to prick with tears. She had to get out of this!

"Aaah!" she jerked, out of necessity for survival, in such a way that her hands were now free, and all she could think to do was struggle all the more, her arms cartwheeling, as she tried to escape this new pain. The leather felt like it was slicing into her! "No, no, no!" she yelped. "No, no..."

Taric was suddenly crouched in front of her, gathering her hands into his own. His expression was oddly patient, and he watched her expression change. In turn, his face began to look not sympathetic, really, but warm. It was quite an odd contrast.

SMACK! "Please, please..." she whimpered at him. "Help..." Her throat was already sore from yelping. She could feel that any second the dam would break, and she would start crying. There wasn't any stopping it.

SMACK! The leather came down right between her bottom and her thighs. Her whole body flinched violently and, just as she expected, tears began to fall.

Looking straight into the face of the handsome, dark-featured human, she began, smack after smack, to blubber like an infant.

She stopped struggling since it was only wearying her, and low and behold, that's when Draevan finally stopped. He passed Taric's belt back to him, but Taric merely took it, set it across his knee, and then pressed his fingers against her tear-stained cheeks. "You have such a pretty cry," Taric told her in an affectionate, enlightened way, like he was watching a sunset rather than a naked girl who'd gotten her tail blistered.

Draevan hadn't yet released her or let her up, but he rubbed his large palm over her skin before gently tracing a couple of the thick welts on her bottom with his finger.

She couldn't believe that these humans were touching her with their dirty hands, but yet there they were. She whimpered, fearing that too much protest would merely lead to more spanking, which was something she couldn't take.

"Damn beautiful," Draevan said in a low, heady voice. His roving, rubbing fingers then found a place between her legs that hadn't been abused... Nor had it ever been touched; it was that territory reserved for the husband she never planned to have.

"Oh..." The touch of his fingers made a low moan come out of her lips, which she immediately quelled. Her eyebrow puckered with confusion, and embarrassment continued to knot her stomach when she realized that she'd moaned loud enough for either one of these men to hear.

"She's a responsive little thing," Draevan informed his cousin. "Do you think we'll get an elf-wife that's this eager?"

"I'm not eager!" she cried, humiliated beyond belief. "I don't want you to even touch me with your dirty, stupid, human fingers!" Her face burned as hot as her bottom.

His fingers continued to delve deeper into her folds, his movement slick because of the moisture that had immediately appeared when his fingers first went that far south. She bit her trembling lip, squinting, unable to look into Taric's eyes once again and see the appraising look on his face.

His finger stopped delving into her. "By all that's holy,

Taric—she's a virgin!"

"Of course I am!" She didn't know why she was furthering his excitement by saying that, because Draevan groaned with need. "Stop..." When Taric let go of her hands, she opened her watery eyes and saw that Taric's nose was nearly touching her own. Without any further warning, he grabbed her chin in his hand and brought his lips forward to kiss her.

No, kissing really wasn't what this was. His mouth pressed hungrily against her own, his tongue delving deeply into her mouth. She'd never seen kissing quite like that... But then, she had hardly seen any kissing at all in her life!

Bite him! she told herself, but she couldn't do it. In fact, she felt her body soften over Draevan's firm thighs, her body coming alive in a way that it hadn't done before; it was as if she were a stranger in her own body. Her body simply wasn't doing what she willed it to!

Taric pulled back, rubbed her cheek again, and said something in that stupid language she didn't know. Draevan quickly growled something in response; apparently not happy with something that was said. Taric's expression firmed as he looked up at Draevan and continued to argue until Draevan grumbled and she felt him let go of her.

Taric helped her stand and then strapped his belt on as she tried to cover her breasts and her front at the same time. She looked up and narrowed her eyes at the men. "Are you quite done molesting me now?" she seethed.

Draevan took her by the elbow, not firmly, but solidly enough to quell any ideas she might have been brewing up about running away. "Not by a long shot!" he huffed. "We're just saving you for our victory feast."

Her face paled. "You're going to eat me?" she gasped. She would believe anything from them at this point...

"Well, we'll definitely be tasting you..." Draevan said, with mischief in his eyes.

"Draevan," Taric said reproachfully. As Draevan was rolling his eyes at the reproach, Taric reached forward by way of asking for her hand. When she didn't put it into his, however, he merely grabbed her fingers tightly and led her to the ground by their saddles where they had been resting. He pulled out a spare shirt and unfolded it by whipping it through the air before handing it to her. Eagerly, she put her hands through the sleeves and into the fabric. It was even larger than the last one—Taric's tunic fell far past her knees. She wrapped her arms in front of her for more warmth.

Taric kicked his and Draevan's leather bedrolls together with the edge of his boot. "You'll sleep here tonight," he informed her, pointing to the bedrolls. "In the morning we'll find a safe place to tie you until after we've dealt with the giant."

She looked at the sleeping area with disgust. Sleep with them? Were they insane? "No!" she refused firmly.

"Did you enjoy your spanking, she-elf?" he asked her.

Immediately her heart hammered at full-speed. She swallowed, but then shook her head.

"Well," he said, "we *did* enjoy ourselves. So please keep that in mind before you speak. Now lay." He pointed to the ground again, and this time she lowered herself obediently to the thick leather roll. Her haunches ached, and she had to adjust herself to her knees, pulling the edge of the shirt over as much of her body as possible. Taric dropped himself next to her, put an arm around her chest, then lowered the rest of his body down and drew a blanket over them.

They were now spooning. She was spooning a human. What was next? Pigs flying? Perhaps a unicorn would walk on by?

What was worse was when Draevan laid down next to her, his face just across from hers, and pulled his own blanket over them so that she was now snuggly under two. She realized that she was now being *sandwiched*.

When she was a true elfling, she would sometimes crawl into her brothers' bedrolls with them on cold nights or when she'd had a bad dream, ignoring how angry they used to get with her afterwards. But this was close to two men, not just one at a time, and Taric already had his arm slung over her waist, his nose buried in her snow-white tresses.

"You smell delicious," Taric told her dreamily, the firmness that had been in his voice just a minute ago completely dissipated.

A sob shook at her shoulders for a moment, startling even her. It wasn't expected, nor could it be helped. It dawned on her, suddenly, that she would not leave until they gave her permission to go… Which might never be. Certainly, they didn't seem to be in any sort of rush to leave her company.

In response, the men's embraces on her merely grew tighter. "You should really just let me go. You can't tie me up," she begged. "You'll die, and then I'll be stuck!"

"Firstly," Taric replied, "that won't happen. We wouldn't have journeyed all the way out here if we weren't absolutely certain that we could defeat the giant. Secondly, you're a thief. Your life is forfeit to your victims, namely us, and it would be too much of a waste to hang you from the nearest tree."

She couldn't tell if he was teasing her or not; his tone could make her believe either way.

Draevan patted his blanket over her hip and said, "Are you warm enough, elfling?"

She curled her frozen toes. "Boots would help," she assured crisply.

He didn't grumble at her terse words, only rubbed his thumb across her cheek. "Yes, but not having them would slow you down if you ran off," he replied wisely. He surprised her by reaching down, grabbing her feet, and warming them in his hands, creating friction with his fingers. He squinted at her, seeming to be evaluating her looks. "You're all by yourself out here, aren't you?" he finally asked with a pitying tone. He didn't even wait for her to verify it before he asked, "How long?"

What was it to him? Was he truly trying to get on her good side after just spanking her and sticking his fingers into a place no man had touched before? "None of your business," she snapped, yanking her foot out of his hands and trying to make sure they were well-wrapped in the blanket.

He didn't look too despondent by her snappishness. Instead, he acted as if she had just spilled her heart out. "Well, don't you worry yourself, elfling. We'll take care of you."

Her lips pursed together, and she growled in threat, "Ditto."

They both snorted out a laugh, and then she felt Taric's hand rub against her hip. The men spoke over her head in that mysterious language.

"What are you called, girl?" Taric asked in her ear.

She didn't answer, merely turned her head towards her pillow. He grabbed her sore ass roughly with his strong fingers, and she gasped, "Kyra Kingsguard!"

Draevan grinned and entwined his legs into hers; she could finally call herself warm from head to toe. "Rest well, our Kyra," he told her, reaching up to pet her hair. "Our cute little thief."

She was certain that it was an impossibility to sleep in these conditions, and she stifled a frustrated growl. She was used to resting with damp, dirty earth under her body, but she wasn't used to the warmth blanketed by the presence of the two men. Yet, not even five minutes later, the warmth from their bodies began to lull her. In a short time, she drifted off into a deep sleep.

CHAPTER TWO

Draevan was beginning to fancy himself in love, which he had never done before. But then, he had never let himself feel any sort affection for any female who wasn't kin before. Since they were small boys, he and Taric had known they would be the ones to kill the giant of Blue Forest and marry the she-elf given to them in payment. Draevan's mother had foreseen that herself, and she was never wrong.

So he never believed he would take one of the women from the village as a wife, and he never let himself grow attached to any woman who warmed his bed, even in the smallest measure.

Now, this fair little lady tucked against his chest, purring in her sleep like a kitten might, warmed not just his body. She was the cutest girl he'd ever seen, and being such made his chest tighten with feeling. Best of all, little Kyra was an elf, which meant that he could marry her all he wanted. After killing the giant, they'd have first pick of any she-elf in the kingdom! It had been long decreed!

Why not pick Kyra? He could already imagine her purring against him every night, and at the mental picture of it, a small grin sprawled on his face. Taric also seemed quite pleased with her; surely Draevan wasn't the only one already baking up fantasies about breeding her—taking her over and over again, filling her with their seed until she birthed not just one, but several sons for them.

Lords, the image alone of her filled with child was already making his cock stiffen uncomfortably in his trews... It seemed like his body wanted that image every bit as much as his mind did. His most basic instincts wanted to claim this girl as his mate, to protect her, to provide for her...

Hopefully Taric shared those feelings.

Because he and Taric had always known they would share a wife, which was not uncommon to Northern villagers, they'd long-ago promised each other that they would take their wife in a way that would make it impossible to tell whose child she bore, and they would love their wife's children as their own.

"Taric?" he hissed over the sleeping girl's head.

Taric made a groaning noise and cuddled closer against her, breathing deeply into the girl's hair. The elfling was small enough that Draevan was able to kick in the space under her and reach Taric's boot with his own to rouse him. "Taric!" he struggled to keep his voice to a whisper, keeping the deep vibration out of his voice so as not to wake her.

"Meh..." Taric grumbled as he stirred. In another second Taric's head darted up in alarm. "Do you hear something?" he asked, as if an approaching giant would be the only reason Draevan would ever wake him.

"No," Draevan said, and Taric's head plopped right back against the saddle and he closed his eyes. Draevan quickly broke into their secret language. *"Taric, I want to keep her."*

"Of course we're keeping her," Taric responded wearily.

"No. I mean, after today... I want to choose her for our mate."

Taric opened his eyes and a long wrinkle appeared across his forehead.

"You're quite bewitched by her, then?" Taric wasn't as judgmental as Draevan feared he'd be. Taric was, by far, the more skeptical of the two, and always stepped in to play the part of devil's advocate. *"I have no arguments. She has no fault a firm hand couldn't remedy. She's beautiful, she smells nice, and I think she's entertaining enough. She'll do."* He shifted and rubbed his hand against the girl's tummy. *"Well, I'm glad I talked you into waiting to take her, then. Call me a romantic, but a bride should be taken on her wedding night."*

Draevan had been finger-deep in her when Taric suggested that they wait until after the giant to bed her, mostly because he didn't want to risk being interrupted and also because he hoped that they'd be better received by her if she knew them as skilled warriors, not just hopeful or even big-headed ones. Draevan had grumbled about it at first, certainly, but now he was quite pleased to have something to look forward to. Besides, Taric had been right to say that the timing wasn't right. Draevan had given her quite the chastisement, and she was feeling molested and forlorn already. He wanted to have her see them as something other than her rapists.

He hummed happily and then snuggled the girl closer to his chest, kissing her forehead. In her sleep, she began to purr even louder.

"We need to rise," Taric reminded him, now that the sun was beginning to shine through the trees. *"We have to hone our blades yet."* Still, he hadn't moved from his place on Kyra's other side.

Draevan grumbled a curse under his breath but slowly got up, feeling cold on the side that had been pressed to Kyra's body. He tucked his cloak closer around her so that she wouldn't have to feel the cold of the morning either, and her body balled up more into the fetal position as she continued slumbering on.

When Taric finally rose, Draevan popped a bannock into his mouth and handed one to Taric, punching him in the rib with his elbow and then nodding to the girl. *"Look at her, sleeping like an angel there...*" He shook his head appreciatively. "*Damn fine find.*"

"*Now if only we can get her to think likewise...*" Taric murmured.

"*Why, is that urgent?*" Draevan asked, shrugging his shoulders. "*She doesn't have to like us. We'll make sure she's satisfied. She'll come around, and if she doesn't... Well, who cares? I'm decided on her, and that's all that concerns me.*"

Taric sighed and raised a dark, judgmental eyebrow. "*Your Northerner is showing,*" he told him, meaning that Draevan was acting particularly brutish.

"*Remember, Grandfather said girls don't often know what's best for them. She's better with us than here alone, in the woods, with a dagger strapped to her calf, and only a handful of coin to her name.*" Draevan swiped his hand confidently through the air, ending the discussion. Taric looked thoughtfully at him, then down at the elf. In moments, he looked approving enough towards Draevan's point by raising his eyebrows and nodding to himself.

They hadn't been honing their blades for five minutes when they first heard the distant sound of thunder, although by the unrelenting way the sun was shining through the thick canopy of winter branches, they could tell that it was a clear, sunny day above.

Another quiet rumble vibrated through the wood of their boot soles. Still, fear didn't cling to Draevan. He could tell that Taric, although he didn't look bored like he usually did, didn't have any look of dread about him either, and this was a man who broke into a flop sweat when he was asked to do any public speaking or when a comely lass would ask him to dance!

Taric then suddenly looked very uneasy when he glanced at the elf-girl who still nestled under a light heap of blankets. "*We chose a poor day to put someone else into our plans,*" Taric sighed. "*I don't want the fight to come too close to her; I worry about tying her down here.*"

Draevan squinted. "*What are our options, Oh-Wise-One?*"

he asked, rolling his eyes dramatically. *"She'll run away. Our little thief is not one to be trusted!"*

Taric shrugged. *"I know it. I just worry for her. I want her to be able to get away."*

"Yes, well, that's exactly what I don't want."

The horses startled, and when they did, Kyra awoke. They could tell immediately, even before she budged, by the way the purring ceased. Another moment later, she was sitting up and pushing the blankets off of her. "The giant's coming!" she fretted, true worry seeping into her eyes.

Damn it all, Draevan hated seeing worry on that sweet little face. He hated seeing the girl he chose as a wife fear *anything*. Draevan himself would swim through a sea of fire to keep her from harm. Slaying a giant was a mere trifle. "Don't worry, we'll take care of it. We're leaving now," he said, grabbing some rope. "That way we can keep him as far away from this camp as possible. We'll come back to you when it's done."

Her eyes found the rope in his hand instantly and gasped. "Don't tie me up!" she begged, reaching up at him and grabbing his hand. "Please, *please* don't."

He shook his hand free of her grasp. "Sorry, but you won't sway me," he told her. "Now come here."

She got to her feet and scurried to Taric now, clasping his forearm tightly. "Please, I'll do anything! I can't be tied up! I'll be eaten! I won't stand a chance!" she fretted at him. "He'll use me as a toothpick to help get you out of his teeth!"

"If we don't tie you, you'll run," Taric said somberly.

"I won't," she promised immediately. "I won't run. I swear, I'll stay right where I am. I swear on my life—I swear on my brothers' lives, I swear on everything I've ever had, that I won't run unless the giant is in view! But if... If you fail... Then..."

Taric turned and looked at Draevan, one of those stupid looks on his face.

"*No*," Draevan snapped, swooshing his hand through the air. "*Absolutely not.*"

They didn't have long to argue about it. The footsteps were getting nearer.

"*If we marry her, we have to be able to trust her,*" Taric tried to rationalize.

Draevan was in no mood for this sort of logic. "*I already trust her. I trust her to run. She'll run, Taric. Tell her no.*"

Taric pressed his lips together, his eyes wondering to the side like they normally did when he was just going to do what he wanted.

"*Tell her no, Taric,*" Draevan hissed.

"*I have a good feeling that she'll stick around.*" A good feeling? Taric's feelings were shit! He had no talent when it came to feelings about people! What was he thinking? "*It will be good for our relationship,*" Taric added, as if he knew anything about relationships. Draevan knew for a fact that he had even less notable experience with women outside of the bedchamber than Draevan did, which was none. "*Let me make this call,*" he pleaded, apparently very aware that Draevan had never denied a direct request from him.

Draevan swore angrily and threw down the rope in his hands.

"You have to swear," Taric told her firmly, turning to see hopeful, happy eyes shine back at him.

"Oh, I do!" She made a show of crossing her heart. "I swear it! You can trust me, honest!"

Draevan sighed, knowing that there was nothing to be done about it now. He wasn't going to be the one to tie her to a tree after her hopes had been risen. He walked up to her and ignored her fearful look at his approach. One day, if she was still around when they returned, he hoped to remedy her fears and have her grow to trust him. Maybe even love him… Despite what he might have told Taric, he realized that the idea of a loving wife was appealing.

He grabbed her waist and yanked her to his chest. "Give us a kiss for luck, then."

She swallowed and hesitated.

"Come on now," he ushered, his expression stern. He waved his fingers impatiently in front of her nose. They had to hurry.

She finally got up on her tiptoes and kissed him. It seemed she was only interested in maybe giving him a peck on the cheek. Instead, he grabbed her tight and forced his mouth onto hers, kissing her deeply. Lords above, did she taste good! He could kiss her forever.

When he let go, she had trouble finding her footing and wavered in her steps. He held her steady, proud to have caused her to lose her balance, and then turned to go.

Taric quickly grabbed her hand, then kissed the side of her neck, eventually finding her lips. He acted as if he were much more tender and lover-like than Draevan was, causing Draevan's face to heat. He knew that Taric would never attempt to get any woman they shared to like him more, and normally he wouldn't care. This time, however, he wanted even-footing.

After kissing her, Taric gave her a peck on the nose, saying, "Be good, now. We'll be back directly, and we'll expect you not to have wondered off."

"Alright," she said, nodding very anxiously, wide-eyed.

Draevan grumbled and then growled, "Be here," before grabbing his war hammer, turning towards the woods, and putting his 'game face' on. He couldn't be distracted, not even by thoughts of her.

He only prayed that she'd keep her word.

* * *

Draevan's mother had predicted that they'd be able to kill the giant, the same one that was presently pounding heavily through the woods, when Draevan was about five and when Taric was around two and a half, which was why they were sent to be raised by a curmudgeonly old general who trained them for this moment since they were old enough to hold a sword.

Actually, he was teaching them before they were really old enough to wield a sword. To this day, thirty years later, Taric always thought that if he was walking around without his sword and satchel, that the old man would pop out of nowhere and switch the lights out of him, even though he'd been dead for ten years.

That being said, when they watched the trees fall and rattle in front of them and realized that the giant was—well, a giant—Taric had the most awful feeling that all the training and beatings in the world couldn't have truly prepared him to fight this fifty-foot monstrosity who was made out of stone and, for all he knew, would eat full-grown men as an appetizer.

"Maybe we should have just taken her," was all he said to Taric about his doubt. They might not ever get another chance!

Draevan shook his head, pursing his lips, watching their enemy stomp closer. "Doesn't matter. I'm going to go back there and marry that girl before morning, so help me." Suddenly he winced. He had never been so set on not-just-fucking a girl before in his life, and he seemed to realize this as much as Taric did. "I mean, it doesn't matter," Draevan recovered, "because we'll have her soon enough." He looked up as the giant peered right at them with muddy-red eyes from the last layer of trees in front of them.

The giant sniffed loudly and grunted aggressively. Birds abandoned their perches and flew up into the sky. It was said that a giant was only as large as its treasure and that it grew as its treasure grew.

If that was true, this was one rich son-of-a-bitch.

Draevan sighed and shook his head. "This is gonna get messy," he stated, pulling out his war-hammer and balancing the weight in his arm.

"It will certainly be an interesting morning," Taric agreed, pulling the second sword out of a satchel strapped to his back.

The giant wasn't the take-prisoners type. He was a smash-now-and-ask-questions-later type of creature. His hand whipped out, coming down like a falling bolder to Draevan and Taric's position. They feinted without trouble, which was something the giant didn't expect by the way it snorted, "Huh?" They then jumped on his wrist like a couple of angry fleas, leaping up his arm right towards his head with great speed.

The armies of the North had a name for them—*Storm Dealers*. It was said that they hit so hard that a crack of their blade actually sounded like a clap of lightening. They had been trained as children to cut through *rocks* if they had to.

Taric, feeling a surge of adrenaline wrack through his body, immediately went and sliced off the giant's ear, causing a mighty roar to shake the forest, and then he slid down the giant's back as a hand came up to smash him like a bug.

"Ho!" Draevan shouted, avoiding several hand-smacking furies. The giant probably looked from a distance like he was trying to get a hornet out of his jacket. "Taric! He's a humpback!"

It shouldn't have been that easy.

As Taric avoided an incredibly narrow escape in which he was nearly pinched up between two fingers, he realized it wasn't easy, but a knot of spine was a target. That is, if the spine on a giant worked like it did on anything else...

Taric looked back just quick enough to see what Draevan was talking about. He was right—there was a hump. "You get the spine. I'll distract him so you don't get squashed!"

"For a big fucker, he sure does move fast!" Draevan hooted by way of agreement as he continued to avoid the giant's hands. "By the way, if something happens to you, I will have no trouble fucking that little fox back there by myself. So if I were you, I wouldn't do anything stupid!"

"Thanks for the warning!" Taric barked back, then leapt up onto the giant's bare scalp, leapt down it, and jumped onto his long, out-hanging nose. Taric grabbed a piece of eyebrow to keep from falling off the edge—which would have been a sure death since he would have been smashed if he hadn't fallen completely.

With his other hand, he swung down and launched the blade straight into the giant's eye.

A piercing screech sounded through the air as the giant screamed in agony, moving his hands to his face. Taric only just missed the scraping hands, leaving his sword in the giant's eye to jump onto his shoulder, then his elbow, and then onto a nearby tree.

The tree branch unfortunately snapped, and Taric found himself free-falling a good twenty feet into a bush.

CRUNCH! CRUNCH! CRUNCH! Another groan sounded above Taric, and it sounded like a thousand trees were cracking and breaking around him. Sore, stunned, and quite prickled, he climbed out of the bush and looked up into the sky, realizing that to live he was going to have to run very quickly to the left, which he did, getting out of the way just before the giant fell flat on his face.

When that happened, the ground shook so violently that Taric still got tossed backwards another six feet. When he landed, he raised his head, checking to see where his cousin was.

He couldn't see Draevan anywhere for a moment, and he whirled around. "Ah!" he shouted, stepping back, not realizing Draevan was right next to him.

Draevan looked like he had split an eyebrow, and he had blood dripping down his nose. But the injury didn't keep him from grinning. He took his sword from his satchel, and Taric got out his spare. "And now," Draevan said, grinding his teeth at the giant writhing weakly on the ground, with a broken back and a stabbed eye, "for the messy part."

The massive undertaking it was to cut off a giant's head

was something that Draevan and Taric had planned to forget as soon as possible. But forgetting was easy once they realized where the giant's treasure was.

In his bones were gold, gems, and jewels packed strongly together. They looked at the severed spine, wiped the blood dazedly off their faces, and then continued to gawk. No wonder giants got bigger when they took treasure—they were *made of it*.

"It like... It's like one of those toys at children's parties. Only full of gold rather than candy," Draevan said, moving closer.

Taric pursed his lips at the description. "Yeah, Draevan," Taric said sarcastically. "Just like that." He rolled his eyes until something caught his eye. He kicked the thick giant's blood away from the ground with the heel of his boot and saw a sharp, golden edge peer through the red. He reached down and, heaving, was able to pick it up.

It was a giant, round shield. Diamonds radiated from it, glittering through the red stain.

Draevan turned. "Is that what I think it is?"

"The elven king's shield?" Taric replied, looking at it. "The giant was wearing it as a necklace." He smirked. "We have our gold, Cousin, we have our shield, and we already have an elven wife with hair like mountain snow and tits like pillows." He wiped his blood-stained face on his sleeve again. "Could this day get any better?"

"Yeah," Draevan grumbled. "To actually have her there when we get back to camp."

"Something tells me she'll be there," Taric said, unable to think about relinquishing this feeling of completeness he felt. "Come on, let's head back. We can get some dwarves out here to get the gold and tell the elves this eve."

"She'd better be," Draevan grumbled. "Because I do not want this moment spoiled."

Taric laughed and patted Draevan on the back. "Don't be so full of doubt."

* * *

"The lying *whore*!" Draevan snapped, wiping the blood out of his eyes as he came to the campsite and realized that not only was the elf gone, but so was his horse. He had never been so upset in his life.

He was going to marry her, for gods' sakes! And she just left. No note, no message, no nothing. She hadn't even wanted to give them farewell kisses... Which he was far less than surprised by, but more horrifically impressive was how well she was able to look straight into their faces and lie.

He threw down his war hammer and turned to Taric to accuse him of being at fault.

Taric's mouth was pressed together so tightly that his lips were turning white. When Draevan opened his mouth to begin blaming him for this current trouble, Taric waved him away, snapping, "I don't want to hear it!"

Draevan clenched his jaw, crossed his massive arms across his chest, and glared at his cousin as darkly as possible. He was not only angry with Taric for losing their girl, but also at himself for letting Taric override him.

They had a lot to discuss before they shared a wife, apparently, or else they wouldn't have one at all! "I can feel your look," Taric hissed, waving Draevan away.

"We could have been filling her with our child this very night, Draevan. She could have given birth nine months from today the future hero of the North, but *no*. No, you just had to run your little experiment!" Draevan yelled. "You can't have realistically thought that our prisoner would just sit on her hands and wait for us to come back!"

"We had to try to trust her," Taric said, but didn't back up his statement with the reason why this level of trust was so important. In the past, when they'd heard that trust was so important in a relationship, Draevan remembered that the advice was normally directed at the wife rather than the husband.

"Damn little thing's invisible, Taric! She's as light on her feet as a dove! We couldn't find her yesterday, and we're not going to find her today! We won't be able to find her until she wants to be found! You damn fool! Next time I suggest we tie a girl up, we're tying her up!"

Taric was always skilled at optimism, so it wasn't too surprising that he was trying to cover up his judgmental snafu now. "It's not like we don't have other options," he said. "We killed the giant, now the elf king owes us a wife of our choosing. That's the decree. I'm sure in the kingdom there are elves that are even more fetching. You think that here—in the middle of a dangerous wood—we'd find the most beautiful girl in the world as a trickster thief out to mock us and steal our coin?"

Draevan ground his teeth but hoped he was right.

* * *

It didn't take very long for both men to find out that Taric was, very unfortunately and very thoroughly, wrong.

It didn't take long to get an invitation to the elf kingdom; the dwarves they'd hired to bring their riches safely back to their village in the North—at a whopping seven percent of profits—somehow told the proper people.

They were the first humans in history invited into the elf kingdom of Alanar, where they presented the king the shield that the giant had worn around his neck until the two men had chopped it off, which had been lost to the elves for nine centuries. The extremely obnoxious king kept his word, but when he told them to choose a bride for themselves, they hesitated, despite the fact that the prophecy was so close to being at-hand.

The elf-women's hesitancy to even be in the same room with Draevan and Taric wasn't why they were having trouble choosing a bride. The problem was that, upon entering the elven kingdom, they realized that the elves were... strange-looking. The little elf woman they'd met in the woods had been the most human-looking of any they'd seen and therefore was the most attractive.

Everything they'd heard about elf women before had been proven to be irreparably true. Kyra had unfortunately been the exception. She must have been too low-born not to have dozens of piercings in her ears, nose, eyebrows, lips, or even her forehead like all the royals had. Everyone in the kingdom seemed rich enough to gorge themselves on Guju fruit, which had stained everyone's teeth—men and women alike—a terrifying blood red, but she was probably too poor to afford to eat them. Kyra apparently hadn't "achieved" anything either, because if she had, she would be nearly covered in tattoos from fingernail to eyelid, which they learned were gained in special ceremonies.

After all of this, the women didn't want to marry *them*. When Taric or Draevan came around the corner, they had the ability to clear a room quicker than if the giant himself had walked by. Still, the men were told to stay in the kingdom as the king's honored guests until a decision was made, and they weren't hurried to make the decision at all. In fact, the elves thought the idea of one of their women mating with either of the men disgusting, and not something to be happy about, let alone be rushed into. Taric and Draevan found themselves heartily agreeing with them.

A week into their visit to the kingdom, however, the men were already beginning to despair about their situation. They had hoped to find another girl like Kyra, and after searching high and low the entire week through the entire elf kingdom, they came up empty-handed.

Taric was becoming more and more uncomfortable by the day. Every single empty minute between the men was tense and filled with accusation. It seemed like the more she-elves they met, the angrier Draevan became, since none of those women were Kyra.

Taric understood Draevan's anger, because he was just as angry with himself. He should have tied her up, simply put. He shouldn't have trusted her.

One day, after searching through the city one last time, they sat in their chambers eating a dinner that was laid out for them, and Draevan suddenly had enough.

"That's it!" Draevan finally said, stabbing the knife he had been distractedly playing with through the thick table in front of him. "We're going to find that lying little slut! If we can kill a giant, we can find a flute-playing, pint-sized brat!" He got up and charged through the room towards his belongings.

Taric was far from arguing. In fact, a wave of relief washed over him. He leapt up from his seat. "And when we find her…" He shook his head. "I'll make sure we keep her. I'll never go against your decisions again."

Draevan sighed and shook his head. "No, it was an honest mistake," he admitted. "If I didn't want her so damn badly, I might have trusted the little brat myself. She made quite a show about swearing on the life of her kin and all that."

Taric let out a relieved breath and nodded, smirking. "It doesn't matter, Draevan. We'll find her." He turned to his packing for this little hunt they were planning. "And when we do, I'm going to tie her to the goddamned bed for the rest of her life!"

Nothing came of his boasting, however, and they spent the entirety of the next month combing the Blue Forest for her. They found some people who had seen her, some witnesses that said they'd even found where she'd sold Draevan's horse, but they found no leads to her whereabouts. They returned to the elf kingdom crestfallen. Draevan hadn't said a word of grief towards Taric since they'd left to search for the girl, but somehow that only made not finding her that much worse. Taric couldn't help feeling ashamed about being so ridiculously trusting of a girl who surely hated them.

Upon their return, they found they couldn't get over the strange morbidity of the kingdom's decorations, which were hanging on lamps and towers. They enquired, after seeing the fifth banner of a skeleton hanging from a scaffold, what the devil was going on.

They'd asked an elf boy, who rolled his young eyes at them both and replied pedantically, "It's Hanging Day! *Of course!*"

"Hanging day?" Taric echoed, furrowing his brows.

"Aye! Hanging Day! It's when all the prisoners in the dungeons are hung! One by one!" He tugged his collar and stuck out his tongue to impression the gruesome manner of death. "Everybody's going to go and watch and feast—it's a holiday."

Taric and Draevan walked away and towards the castle, peering at each other. "Elfkind are strange folk," Taric finally decreed, but then his shoulders slouched when he realized, with much horror, that he would have to marry one of them. "I'm beginning to think the fate of the world isn't our problem. Let's just go home and enjoy our treasure."

"We can escape the kingdom, maybe. But we can't escape our fate, Taric," Draevan reminded, his voice pained. "It's foretold—the chosen one will be half giant-slayer and half-elfkind. Unfortunately, I cannot think of any other giants, or of anyone who's ever slain any... 'Tis too late. We can no sooner keep the sun from rising."

Taric grunted unhappily, cursing his own name.

When they walked into the castle, they were told that the king requested audience with them upon their return. They were led out to the festival yard in the back of the castle, where everyone was beginning to assemble for the hangings. The king had never looked happier, his smile never redder, his piercings particularly shiny. They could almost be fooled that the king was happy to see them return, but they feared the king really just liked a good, entertaining execution.

Only an elf would view an execution like a normal person would view a picnic on a sunny spring day. Thinking about it, the only time when Draevan or Taric had ever heard of an elf being seen was when a village execution was going on. They'd heard in the nearby villages that elves would sometimes appear to watch and then leave afterwards with a spring in their step.

"Did you take care of your business, lads?" the king asked them, chortling.

"As best we could," Draevan grumbled and plopped heavily down in the seat the king offered him. There was a turkey leg on the platter in front of him that he made quick work of as the king offered his condolences to their mood and then began to crow merrily about the hangings that were coming about.

"You see," the king told them, "because of you lads, it's a larger event than it's ever been! Because the giant's dead, we were able to clean the untouchable thieves out of the Blue Forest and beyond! Now that there's no true danger of the giant, the bounty-hunters and royal guards have been busy bees all month long; they've been bringing back carts and carts full of thieves, murderers, poachers—you name it. I even have a couple of *beheadings* scheduled!" He clapped his hands together with excitement.

"Oh, goodie," Taric sighed into his freshly-poured chalice of wine.

Even though they had definitely delivered their fair share of death—hell, maybe even *because* of it—Taric and Draevan were never excited to see one man after another succumb to justice. Some of their friends were forced to go to every execution growing up in their village, their fathers thinking it would teach them some sort of lesson. The only lesson their own grandfather had seen fit to teach them was that life was crueler than it needed to be. He never made them go, and so they rarely had gone.

Once the king announced to a ready crowd for the

'festivities' to commence, Draevan and Taric noticed that the worst part of a hanging wasn't the actual death. What was by far worse was the amount of groveling the poor victim would do before he was ignored and dragged up to the scaffold.

After two, even Draevan, who normally let his stomach dictate his morals before his brain was given the opportunity, had quite lost his appetite. "Excuse me, Your Highness," he grumbled, standing from his seat. "We are tired from the journey, so we'll have to excuse ourselves…"

The king frowned. "Oh?" he said, disappointed. "But you're my honored guests… And it's just begun!" He had the look of a man who was insulted. Apparently, he was proud of this event.

"Well, the thing is…" Draevan began to say, before he was cut short as a boy with muddy, bare feet and wearing a bag on his head was led out towards the king to get his death sentence. Needless to say, the sad sight broke Draevan's train of thought.

There was a sack on the boy's head, just like with every criminal led out, but this time when the boy was 'unveiled', the crowed hummed with excitement.

Taric's breath hitched. It wasn't a boy at all! It was *Kyra*; her coat had hid her curves, and the sack had hid everything else, even her ivory hair that was knotted messily to the back of her neck. Dirt and soot blackened whole patches of her skin, and she stood shivering in the cold, winter air. She looked like she had spent a very hard, long month in the dungeons.

Taric and Draevan watched her with their mouths open wide enough for a bird to perch on their tongue. They heard what the king was saying, "Well, well! The last of the infamous Kingsguard family finally meets its end!" he gloated. "After your brothers had a short-drop-and-a-sudden-stop, I thought you would have been gobbled up by the giant soon after!"

"Well, I'm glad my family could entertain you one last time," she replied, spitting with disdain.

"Me as well! Farewell, Lady Kingsguard!" the king waved his hand, and the executioners grabbed her arms to drag her up the scaffold towards the noose.

Moving as one, Draevan and Taric didn't even plead to the king. Their first thought was to get her safe.

They jumped over the rail and pounced onto the ground fifteen feet below. Draevan had his sword unsheathed and raised high above his head, and the executioners stared at him with horror in their pale yellow eyes. They wouldn't fight him—elves were cowardly where battle was concerned. "Drop her," Draevan hissed, and the executioners immediately dropped her arms and showed Draevan their hands. Elves, after all, loved executing but hated fighting.

When she was released, it was with a motion that made her topple into Taric.

The king stood up on his feet and put his hands on the rail in front of him. "What's the meaning of this, Giantsbane?" the king demanded, looking more aghast than angry. He was using the name that he'd given them when they'd first come into the kingdom. The crowd around them was certainly excited.

"This girl is under our protection," Taric replied wrapping his arm tightly around Kyra and holding her to his chest. Surprisingly, she didn't try to escape him. In fact, her nails were digging desperately into his arm, and she was trembling. The brave face she had displayed in front of the king was a farce. She had been horrified by her impending death.

"This girl is a wanted criminal from an old family of traitors and thieves!" the king argued firmly and loudly enough for everyone to hear. "She's an untouchable outcast! The noose is really too good for her kind!"

"We choose her as wife!" Draevan firmly and loudly decreed.

The king was so surprised that he took a step back. The crowd loudly tittered and guffawed around them. "Her?" the king asked, looking like he was unsure that he'd heard Draevan correctly. "*Her*?" he echoed. "You'd take her as wife? Out of anyone? You can have your choice of anyone in the kingdom..." he explained, which was silly of him, since he wasn't excited about giving any elf-woman to them at all, and certainly wouldn't have ever promised one to them if he hadn't been so desperate to have someone kill that giant to get his precious shield back.

"If you will bid us a boon and pardon her, Your Highness..." Taric said, puffing out his chest. He was ordinarily horrified of speaking in front of crowds, but the girl clawing into his arm with fear was enough to keep his words loud and steady. "We will be more than happy to take her as wife and leave your good ladies to be had only by elf-kind. We have no desire to take a beloved daughter from a father, or sister from a brother." It was a lie, of course. They would have had trouble ever being aroused by any other she-elf!

"The way we see it," he continued, "this is the only way to keep your people from heartbreak and to save a lady from the noose."

"Ah!" the king grinned, nodding. "*Now* I understand! You just don't want to see a female hung! I forgot how soft you humans are when it comes to women's punishments..." He straightened the robe on his shoulders, grinning. "So, I will grant you what you wish, for we owe you much, my lads! Very well! Very well, indeed!" He gave a happy laugh. "Then have your woman; she is pardoned! Kyra Kingsguard will forever be known from here forth as Kyra Giantsbane!" He gestured with his arm. "Bring the marriage chalice, and let's make this official."

Draevan looked back and forth before putting his sword into its sheath. Taric did the same with his own, and they exchanged looks. They were surely thinking the same thing: that this was not a very romantic setting. Two men's bodies were already stacked on the other side of the yard, and many men were waiting their turn with sacks over their faces off to the other side of the stadium.

Draevan pulled Kyra out of Taric's arms so he could put his hands on the sides of her face. Adrenaline was still surging through his veins and reddening his skin. Draevan wanted to ward off any attempts at her throwing a fit and told her firmly, "You are ours now. Do you understand? Ours. You have no choice in this. Your choices are spent." Her lip trembled in reply, and he asked in a softer tone, "Are you injured?"

She shook her head weakly, failing to meet either of their eyes. Taric couldn't decide whether this was because she was tired, terrified, or ashamed.

Draevan took a deep, relief-filled breath but then went right back to being firm. Taric could see that he was still pride-stung from her disappearance and the taking of his horse and his heart along with her. "Good. That's one good bit of luck out of all this. We've been combing the forest for you for a whole month." He sighed and rubbed his hand over his face. "This could have all been avoided, pet, if you just did as you were told. Let this be a firm lesson for you."

The girl started to sniffle, but Taric looked over her head and gave the smallest of guilty grins at Draevan, and Draevan smirked back. He was happy again—they finally had the girl they'd wanted from the beginning.

"*Damn strange creatures*," Draevan grumbled to Taric in their secret tongue. "*Who are we to agree to marry her in this hell?*"

Taric entwined his hand around Kyra's. "*Ones who don't want to wait any longer to bed their wife and leave this horrible place. This is a blessing, believe me!*" Taric was practically laughing when he said it, trying not to let himself realize that if they hadn't seen the king when they did, or if they had left sooner, or if they hadn't given up looking for Kyra when they did, she'd be dead, along with their hopes of happiness.

"Please... Please don't make me marry... I'm just... just..." she murmured, sniffling, unable to reach their eyes.

"Fifteen paces towards death?" Draevan finished, in no mood to broach any argument from her. "I can't believe you'd have the gall to refuse us. We just saved your life. You're marrying us, and that's that. Now shush with your nonsense."

"But—but I can't marry *two men*!" she sobbed.

"You can and you will," Draevan argued.

Taric wanted to wrap her up in his arms and explain that in the Northlands, it was actually quite normal for a wife to take two husbands at once. Because the nobles tended to scoop up many women for their harems, there weren't normally scores of women to go around for the rest of the population. Strangely, it worked out that way—a woman and her children were sure to never to go hungry with two providers, such women tended to be better kept in line, and if the village was raided, she had two protectors, and maybe more depending on the age of her sons.

Draevan and Taric had been honing their skills to kill the giant, knowing there would only be one wife given as their reward. That being said, they were quite resolved to the fact that they would be sharing a wife their entire lives. That idea, however, might have been quite different to a girl from a culture where, although one elf could marry multiple she-elves, it was simply unheard of for a woman to marry more than one man.

The king actually walked down onto the field with the sacred wedding chalice in his hands, set to perform the ceremony for them. He actually seemed friendlier than ever now that it was certain Draevan or Taric wouldn't ask for the hand of one of his daughters or nieces.

During the ceremony, called 'The Binding', the men drank out of the chalice before it was offered to Kyra, who dug in her heels and clenched her lips together.

The king glared at her for a long moment. It wasn't usual for an elven girl to be forced into marriage, but then nothing about this situation was usual. It was unusual to have humans in the kingdom at all, it was unusual to get any sort of pardon from the king, and it was unusual to have an audience of this size at a wedding ceremony. Everyone was watching from the stadium around them.

"Hold her," Draevan ordered Taric, who promptly pinned her hands to the small of her back with his grip. Draevan took the chalice, pinched her nose, and waited for her to open her mouth where the wine from the cup was immediately sloshed into her mouth.

She coughed and sputtered. When Taric let her hands go, she wiped them across her face, muttering something to herself that he couldn't hear. She was trembling again, and then Taric and Draevan both put a hand around one of her upper arms, as if helping her to stand.

The king had a gratified look on his face as he continued the ceremony, as if the force they were using with their bride pleased him in some way.

It was then that the men felt a burning on their skin that stretched from their fingernails to their elbows—Draevan's left arm and Taric's right. This burning began to sear, as if an invisible knife was slicing into them.

Draevan's expression changed to murderous, and he opened his mouth to say something, but a forlorn cry of pain escaped Kyra's lips, and he turned to look at her.

The skin on her arms was beginning to change. While there used to be a small white tattoo spanning up some of her fingers, now the lace-like paisley tattoo began to creep up her skin like a vine, right before their eyes.

"You are bound forever together," the king finished, and then gestured for his people to rejoice. For a long while, Taric and Draevan were too busy inspecting the arms of their new wife to begin inspecting their own. When they looked down at their hands and forearms, they saw that where their own skin had been seared and pained was a tattoo exactly like their wife's.

"What is this?" Draevan asked the king as the people all around them cheered, happy that they weren't the ones who had to marry them.

"The Binding," the king replied, as if the answer was all too obvious. When Draevan remained unhappy by the response, he added, "There's magic binding you together now. You all have become of one spirit, and her powers are now shared by you."

"She cannot turn invisible?" Draevan asked, awed. Somehow they both felt that was the best part of this 'binding' nonsense.

The king looked at him like Draevan was a child fooled by a magician pulling a coin from behind his ear. "She cannot hide from you anymore than you can hide from yourself." The king turned, then looked over his shoulder as if he'd forgotten something. "Congratulations."

CHAPTER THREE

It had been a trying day, and all Kyra wanted to do was vomit what pittance was left in her stomach and curl up into the fetal position in a corner somewhere. Her stomach was tied into knots, and she had barely slept for nearly a month. She was exhausted, cold, and damp because the dungeons had less-than-ideal conditions for those who wanted to stay dry.

Her arms throbbed, and her pride? Well, that was long gone. It had been gone since the night she decided to play with fire in the form of the human giant-killers.

"C'mon, honey," Taric said when she crumpled over before they'd even made it out of the arena. He hoisted her easily into his arms and carried her like a babe up the stairs leading towards the castle.

"Is she alright?" Draevan asked over her head. "God help us if she's taken ill!"

"I don't know. She's cold as ice," Taric replied, concern saturating his voice. He looked down at her. "What were you thinking about, running away? We told you we'd take care of you from here on out."

"I'm not..." She meant to argue that she wasn't a slave, that they didn't own her, and a lot of other trifle that, since the binding ceremony, wasn't at all true. Wives, when looked at it in a certain way, were very similar to slaves. They had to do what they were bid; their husbands kept all the rights of their person.

She didn't get to even argue. She passed out. She had never fainted before, but then again, she had never been nearly hung and then married to two human men against her will before. Though the real reason she'd fainted was mainly because she hadn't been given water or food for the last three days because the executioners preferred a clean corpse, and before that, the bowls of gruel she had been eating the last three weeks weren't the most nutritious meals she'd ever eaten.

When her eyes fluttered open, she found herself lying in a *bed*. She had never lain in a bed before; and it was just like she'd heard it to be. It was like sleeping on cloud! Even though her head and stomach ached, she could still feel the fluffy mattress under her, pleasantly warm.

It was then she realized she had been... bathed. Her body felt so clean and soft, and she smelled good, fresh.

"*Finally!*" she heard a male's voice above her say. The word was pregnant with relief. "She's waking up." She felt a calloused hand press against her cheek. The skin of the hand touching her felt so rough; like a crust of bread. She opened her eyes and saw Draevan above her, his brow wrinkled as he gazed down at her. "Dying after the ceremony is a cheap way to get out of your duties," he told her. As always, his voice and eyes were stern and made her stomach flutter with nerves, but his touch was careful and loving, like she was a small pet.

"Told you she'd be fine," Taric said, leaning over her and glancing at her face. He put a hand under her and hoisted her back up until he replaced his hold with about five pillows to prop her up. *Real* pillows—feather ones. "Even the color's back in her cheeks." He grabbed a mug from a nearby tray and put it into her hands. "Drink this," he ordered her.

His order was so firm, she didn't even sniff the contents first; she just brought it to her lips and drank. Luckily, she discovered it was only lukewarm water. When she was done, Taric took it and filled it again, and then again. Upon the forth cup, she shook her head and pushed it away. "I'm going to start sloshing," she grumbled.

He frowned, but maintained his patience. "Ready for food, then? When was the last time you ate?"

She found it difficult to keep her eyes held up from the bedspread. She raised her shoulders until they hitched near her ears. What had happened before she'd lost consciousness had finally hit her. These were the same men she'd tried to rob, who'd stripped and spanked her before apparently killing the giant of Blue Forest. They were the ones who had shoved their fingers up her virgin entrance and kissed her deeply, saying that she cried prettily.

And they were now her husbands.

"Don't keep us in suspense," Taric said patiently.

"I don't know. Wednesday, maybe." It was Sunday, now. When she told them, Draevan swore and then stood up to pace the room. For reasons unknown to her, she felt pleased by his furious response.

Taric left to go get something and then returned. "Draevan, relax," Taric told him, since there seemed to be a cloud of anger fuming out of him. He came and sat down on the bed next to her hip, peeling the skin from a strange, orange piece of fruit.

She blinked at it. It was an *orange*—she'd never had one of those before. Hell, they were nearly impossible to get this far north; they must have cost a fortune.

"You, little girl, have been the cause of a lot of strife," he told her, but he didn't sound unhappy. "We've been searching for you the last month complete. Luckily, we gave up and came back just before you were able to depart from this place entirely."

"Are you looking for an apology?" Because they

weren't going to get one. "Or are you looking for my *thanks*?" They weren't going to get that, either! They only saved her life to pursue their own dark purposes.

There was a warning behind Taric's dark green eyes, but he merely handed her a juicy slice of orange. "Eat that." She did, mostly because out of the corner of her eye she could see Draevan look at her, and she didn't like his expression. It seemed foreboding, as if he was waiting for her to throw a tantrum.

She was so agitated by her current situation that she nearly forgot to enjoy the delicious juice of the orange slice sliding down her throat. She'd seen them before, but she'd never had the opportunity to steal one and thus hadn't ever tried one. It was astounding how savory the flavor was; her mouth was almost pained by the overwhelming gratification it felt.

Taric continued in a patient tone, but his brow was scrunched with frustration. "I don't know where this aggression from you is coming from, Kyra. *You* stole from *us*. We didn't come looking for you; we were merely in the position to catch you red-handed. And as for your crimes: we had nothing to do with them, your capture, your trial, or your sentencing. I can promise you that being our wife is better than being hung for the entertainment of ten thousand people. If you only do as you're told, you will feel quite spoiled."

'Spoiled' was quite a word for it. It sounded like she was going to be forced to do whatever they willed under threat of a beating. "If I don't, you'll spank me!" she accused, trying to make him feel guilty for what he'd done.

"Of course we will! What else do you expect us to do with a bull-headed little elfling?" he returned, furrowing his eyebrows at her. He handed her another slice of orange. "You no longer have to lie, cheat, poach, or steal any longer. You will be given everything you desire; you only have to be obedient, respectful, and bear us sons."

"You can't just *breed me* like some filly!" she snapped,

red-faced. It was impossible, anyway. She'd never heard of a cross between the two species. They were too different to imagine such a thing.

Taric merely shrugged at that. "We can, actually. Your acceptance of all this is really not required. Whether you enjoy it or not is up to you." He handed her another slice. "But I think you will."

She clenched her teeth, feeling like her whole body was shaking with fury. She seemed to have come across the path of men who were interested in protecting her from everything except themselves!

The worst of it was that she didn't have any other choice. They were her husbands—she was merely a slave to their wishes, and she already knew not to try their tempers. They were larger than her, faster than her, stronger than her, and they would soon be taking what was theirs, which was her body.

She swallowed. "You bathed me, didn't you?" she asked flatly, feeling churlish.

"Draevan and I did, yes," he replied unapologetically. "We wanted to inspect you, anyway, to look for injuries, parasites, and rat bites. You *were* in a dungeon for a month."

"Romantic," she snorted, embarrassed by the act and by his clinical tone.

He smirked. "I thought it *was* incredibly romantic of us. We're your white knights, my dear, right out of a fairy story."

"I've never heard a fairy story that ends with rape," she sneered.

"Well, normally those stories don't have women who are as stubborn as you are."

"Talk about stubborn! Why were you so interested in keeping me, anyway? There's a kingdom full of elves here, you know. You could have had your pick. Why me?"

"You appealed to us."

"Why do you even care? You could have just killed me.

That's normally what people do with thieves. Thieves make poor slaves, you know." She crossed her arms, refusing to take any more orange from him.

"Apparently," he agreed, rolling his eyes. "But we weren't going to kill you. Never had such a thing ever crossed our minds. Draevan has a sixth sense, you know. He can quite read what's in a person's heart."

"That's ridiculous!" she said, aghast. "You're humans! You have no magical ability whatsoever!"

"He's never failed. Gets it from his mother. She was a well-known soothsayer," he told her, his tone resolute. He truly did believe in Draevan's ability... As strange as it sounded. It figured; these men were from the North... The most superstitious realm in creation. Every village there had its own seers, legends, myths, and foretellings. "She knew we'd both come together to slay the giant of the Blue Forest." Well, that explained their confidence in themselves...

"And," Taric added casually, "we chose you because you are the most beautiful woman in the world." He put down the orange peel on the side table. "And we've met *many*."

Her cheeks felt hot when he said that. She had never ever been known as pretty, particularly by anyone who had seen another elf. Her brothers, although they loved her, used to tease that she was so ugly that she could break their looking glass.

Nothing about her was beautiful! Her cheeks were too pink, her eyes were too gold, her lips too red, and her teeth her were too white. She had freckles, which were disgusting, and because she was untouchable and outcasted, she could never find anyone who would touch her long enough to give her a piercing. Tattoos? She only had the ones that showed up on her fingers magically after her family died off one by one. She had nothing about her to attract any sort of a mate!

For a moment, she was sure that he was teasing her,

but the more she looked at him, the more she decided that he was being sincere. They did, for whatever strange reason, think she was pretty.

"Besides, you're appearing like the type of girl who needs two husbands just to keep an eye on you," he added off-handedly, causing the beginnings of her smile to stop in motion. He wasn't noticing; his attention was on Draevan now, who was still stomping around and muttering to himself on the other side of the room. "You okay over there, Drae?"

"*Three days* without food or water? What's wrong with these people?" was the response received. "That's it. I'm getting my war hammer. What I'll do with it, I don't know, but—!" his voice drained out as he stomped into an adjoining room.

Taric sighed and put a hand across her knee and squeezed it lightly. "Drink another cup of water," he told her, handing her the mug she had refused earlier. "And we'll see how well you keep down the bit of orange. I want you to continue to rest and build up your strength for the journey home. I'll be back to watch over you as soon as I get Draevan to calm himself down."

She gave a nod, and he turned his back on her to follow Draevan out to the adjoining room.

Years from now, she would still wonder what she was thinking when she pushed the covers down, tightened the belt around the robe the men had dressed her in, and looked for an escape route.

After all, if she didn't escape, she was looking at a fate far worse than getting her clothes stripped off.

If she could only make it into the woods, she could be safe. Whether or not she could use her magic to hide herself away from them now that they were wed didn't matter—she had grown up in those woods, and she felt she could evade anyone in the maze-like forest. It was astounding that the humans hadn't landed themselves in the ample amounts of quicksand outside of the kingdom yet! But the problem was getting *to* the forest, and for that, she needed an escape route, and there didn't seem to be any good ones that were readily available, save one. The window.

She grabbed at the nearest window and ran her fingers along it. She had seen other people open windows before, but she had never actually done it herself... She'd never had a window to open. Presently, she pulled up on the window pane until it creaked open from the bottom.

A flurry of wet, cold wind carrying a heavy mist blew into the room, and she poked her head outside and looked down. The stone seemed easy enough to scale down, especially after her experiences at rock and tree climbing, but she had never climbed anything that was this high from the ground. The height was enough to make anyone dizzy.

She turned and listened closely to make sure the men were still in deep conversation, yapping back and forth in their strange language. She took a deep breath then and, checking the security of her robe, she carefully reached her legs out the window and began the lengthy climb to the bottom. Not only had she decided that she'd do this, but she'd also decided she'd be on the ground before her husbands realized she was gone.

After she was a good twenty feet below her room's window, she nearly slipped and fell to her death, because the tower was far more slippery than she'd thought it'd be, and her urgency to climb down in a hurry had made her movements jerky and clumsy. She looked down, recognized she still had over a hundred feet left to scale, and promptly felt like a fool. Hugging herself to the wall until her fingers turned white, she was beginning to grumble about how stupid she was. "*Really stupid!*" She took another step, and her foot couldn't find another solid holding. She looked down and decided that, if she fell, she might actually go 'splat!' "I can't do this!" she gasped to herself, trying to keep her body from shuddering. She could feel fear radiating from her body, chilling her even more than the air.

Sex with a couple of human men, she was deciding, on a nice cushy bed, in a nice warm room, for the rest of their lives, surely couldn't be worse than death. Plus, she was an immortal and might even outlive them. Then again, maybe she wouldn't after being bound together in the marriage ceremony—there was also a good probability that they now had the ability to live forever just like any other elf-kin; that's why an elf-wife was such a good catch for a human in the first place!

But it didn't matter. A thousand years as a slave was better than going 'splat' anywhere.

Was it disgusting to lower herself in such a manner to a race below her own, even though she was what the elves called 'untouchable'? Well, yes, of course it was. Still, shame was something she could live with, just as long as it came without the... well, going 'splat'.

"Help me..." she whispered to nobody in particular. She knew her husbands were too far away to hear her and come to her aid, but somehow she found herself too frightened to even make too much noise, as if a scream's vibration would shatter the very stone she was gripping onto for dear life.

"Kyra!"

She closed her eyes, not daring to look up. It was hard enough to claw her fingers into the stone. It didn't change that she was intensely grateful that the men had looked out the window and seen her about thirty feet down and frozen there. Possibly, if they weren't too angry with her, they might even help.

"I'm coming for you. Hold on!" she soon heard Taric's voice promise from somewhere above her. She tried to look up but was rewarded by small rocks and dust falling into her eyes, making her look down again.

Before she could believe it, Taric was next to her with a rope tied around his waist. He moved in a way so that his body covered hers and he slowly helped her peel away from the wall. "This was a poorly planned idea, wasn't it?" he lectured darkly when she turned and latched her arms and legs tightly around him until he was nearly gasping for breath. He looked up, "Alright, Draevan! I've got her!"

The rope pulled them both up, which was surprising. Together, they must have been quite a weight for Draevan, since Taric couldn't have been too much lighter than him, even by himself!

"You could have probably gone right out the front door," Taric grumbled curtly in her ear. "But no. No, you're too clever for that. You had to *scale down the building*. Oh, gods. You are in so much trouble; you can't even *comprehend* how much."

He was half right. She didn't comprehend it right then, perhaps, since she was feeling quite relieved at not having fallen to her death. However, comprehension seeped in as soon as Draevan pulled them through the window. When she saw the dark and animalistic look in his eyes, she actually did grasp how much trouble she was in:

She was in more trouble than she could handle.

* * *

With a final heave, Draevan watched as Taric pushed Kyra up through the tall window where she crawled back into the room. Kyra, her fingers gripping the floor desperately, reminded him of a half-drowned kitten with the way the heavy mist had wetted down her robe and white hair. He nearly forgot about Taric; all Draevan could think about was how much Kyra looked like someone who needed a man's arms around her.

He and Taric had been discussing the proper care of Kyra now that she was awake. She was already surly-tongued with them, but neither of them thought she was in a well enough state to accept any sort of discipline. She hadn't even seemed ready to be made love to!

They had been eager to punish her for running away from them when she'd promised to stay that one day in the forest, but now that they had her for their own, utterly and legally, they didn't feel the urge. Instead of discipline, they had decided that their new wife needed understanding and patience until she could assume her role as their wife. After the ordeal she'd just been through, they figured she needed some tender loving care more so than a firm-handed pair of husbands.

It was so quiet in the next room where they thought Kyra had still been that they'd assumed she was sleeping. They might have talked even longer if Draevan hadn't felt a strange feeling inside his stomach, as if his insides had been doused with ice water. It was a horrible feeling, and when he glanced up from his own abdomen, he saw Taric press his hand against his own stomach, uncannily feeling the same way at the same time.

It had been right then that they looked at each other and knew Kyra was in trouble. How they knew, Draevan couldn't be sure, but the feeling of dread was undeniable. Then they searched through an empty room only to finally recognize a chill coming from an open window that Draevan couldn't even get his shoulders through. Even Taric had barely been able to fit himself outside.

Now, he looked at her, and he felt a warm feeling come into his chest once again. As soon as Taric was half-way through the window, Draevan dropped the rope and rushed to grab ahold of Kyra. Her body was cold from the winter night air and the misty rain, and she was shaking as he held her to him.

Taric closed the window after he'd climbed in and looked at them, flipped some of his dark hair out of his eyes, then crossed his arms over his chest.

As soon as Draevan was assured she was uninjured, anger finally emerged and spread quickly through him. He pulled away from her, and she looked up at him with shiny, fearful eyes. Damn right they were fearful! She had been spanked before by him, and he knew that she wasn't stupid. She had to have known that he was going to make that last spanking look like patty-cake!

Draevan grabbed the fluffy belt around her robe and unknotted it with frustrated movements. She began to try to pull away from him, but he tugged her robe forward until she stood still enough that he could peel the robe off of her slender, pale shoulders,

To say she didn't like being stripped was an understatement. Though they had already seen her naked, even as recently as an hour ago, she fought to keep the hem of her robe closed between her breasts. He quickly lost patience with her struggling and spun her around to land a firm, resounding slap on her round little bottom.

"Behave!" he warned her in a bark that was loud enough to startle her still for a moment, long enough for him to grab her robe and pull it straight off her body until she was standing naked in front of the fire, trying to cover her body as much as possible with her two small hands.

He was upset with her, but even so her beauty in the room's firelight wasn't at all lost on him. She was absolutely gorgeous naked, and he could feel his animalistic urges blister within him, but he ignored them. He would take her soon, but for now, she needed someone to lay down the law. Women needed structure and discipline; it was like his grandfather had always said. So, instead of pulling to the floor and rutting over her until both of them were sweaty and exhausted with satisfaction, Draevan grabbed her wrist and dragged her over to the bed.

Taric didn't say anything, merely trudged behind them supportively. When Draevan forced her up on the bed, she immediately tried to scurry to the far side, closing her hands around her bare, milky white breasts. "Please!" she cried. "I'm sorry! I really am! It was stupid, but I'm sorry!"

"Bend over the bed," he growled, grabbing for his belt. "I am going to beat your ass until it *glows*!"

Her eyes rounded. "No, no!" she cried, putting up her hands. "P-please. I'll be good."

Draevan ground his teeth as he looked up and down her body. His mind was beginning to fill with a million sexy scenarios. It was impossible for him to keep his eyes off of her; the way the lamplight reflected off of her naked skin, her flat tummy, the bend of her waist. He wished he wasn't angry with her. He wished he could just wrap his hands around her waist, push her to the mattress, and feed himself deep into her.

Unfortunately, letting her talk her way out of a good solid strapping was not a good precedent to set for their future. He pulled off the rest of his belt and doubled it over in his hands. "Bend. Over."

"Please no, Draevan. I'm—I'm tired, and I don't feel good…" She lowered her head.

"That's what *we'd* thought! Yet you felt well enough to scale thirty feet down," he argued, pointing towards the window.

She raised her head, her eyes shifting around nervously. She was apparently trying to think fast. She looked over at Taric, who was standing and staring darkly at her, and then back at Draevan. "Then… If I have to get spanked… Can Taric do it?"

Draevan dropped his belt-holding arm down to his side, feeling struck. A wave of emotion swept over him; emotions of jealousy and hate and anguish and self-loathing. Their marriage had barely begun, and she already preferred Taric? Draevan's shoulders slouched forward as he promptly began to pity himself that he'd already given his cousin enough of a foothold to be the more loved husband, one she'd trust more with her punishment, and probably everything else…

Draevan was sure that, when he looked over at Taric, the man would be openly gloating, raising his chin, squaring his shoulders back, and looking very pleased with himself.

That's not what he saw. When he glanced Taric's way, there was a vein pulsing from Taric's neck that he hadn't noticed in his entire life. The man was absolutely livid. Instead of being touched by her preference of disciplinarian, he had instead taken great offense.

Come to think of it now, Draevan realized that the girl, most likely, merely thought Taric to be the more sensitive and weaker one of the two.

Taric was rolling up his sleeves, his lips drawn over his teeth nearly like he was grinning. It was maniacal. "*Let me*," Taric told him. "*Just hold on*."

"*Where are you going?*" Draevan asked, unable to figure it out until Taric soon returned with an ivory phallus in his hands. It was a bottom-plug; the strangest bauble amongst their treasure. Taric had been extremely amused when he'd found it and cleaned it thoroughly, joking that he would eventually be threatening his wife with it. "*Oil that*," Draevan requested with a bit of a sigh.

He didn't want to have to go there with her already; the bottom was supposed to be slowly broken in and savored, preferably well into the marriage when a level of trust had been approached. However, it couldn't be argued that she didn't deserve the shock of it. It would certainly make the punishment more pronounced. Besides, Draevan couldn't help but believe that, although it was nice to have a wife's trust and adoration, it was also good to have her respect and obedience.

She was looking curiously over at Taric, and Draevan grabbed her chin between his fingers. Her attention instantly squared on him. Her eyes were wide and round as he gritted, "Bend over the edge of the bed." He released his hand from her face and gestured for her to be quick about it.

Her eyes darted back and forth nervously, hesitating more and more until he snapped, "Do it now, or so help me…"

He didn't have to finish his threat to get her to believe

him. She promptly turned and lowered her legs from the side of the bed until her pale white bottom was sticking out for both of their eyes to feast upon.

Taric grunted in a way that made Draevan turn his head towards him where Taric was looking dead-straight at her, completely ignoring the bottom-plug he was oiling. Draevan cleared his throat, and Taric snapped back into awareness, but not before giving him an expression that said, '*Have you seen the goods on our wife or what?*'

When Taric approached and waved towards her, Draevan marched over to the far side of the bed and grabbed her hands.

"Arch your bottom out," Taric ordered Kyra, who didn't budge a notch. Her knees bent, actually, which lowered her bottom even more.

"Please—let's just start over!" She was already trying to tug her hands away from Draevan, but he was happy to hold them firmly. She wanted this, he had to remind himself—she hadn't wanted him to punish her. She asked for Taric, so she would get him, simple as that.

Maybe at the end of all this, she would realize that there were worse things than a spanking from him. He wouldn't be surprised if the next time she needed discipline, she'd seek *him* out first.

* * *

Gods above, Taric had never seen a more glorious bottom in all his days. Though, he hadn't seen many. Even when he took a working lady to… well, work on *him*… it was normally full-night, in places where he'd consider himself lucky if there was a candle in the room at all!

But this wasn't just any woman's bottom—it was his. Well, *theirs*… This was his wife's body. This was the bottom that he would be plowing into for the rest of his life. He couldn't wait for his life to begin!

He turned the ivory phallus around in his hand and

stepped forward. If her bottom hadn't already made him hard as a rock, the mere idea of seeing her squirm when she was violated in her most secret place would have. Perhaps it was perverted, but he didn't care; he was going to make her blush down to her toes.

Taric got down on one knee behind her and put his hands on her bottom, gripping his hands on her wonderful, soft flesh. It wasn't lost on him how amazing it would surely feel when he rammed his member into her.

She began to squeal and squirm as he spread her cheeks apart; that was before she even knew what was in store for her. His grip on her became a little punishing as he pressed the head of the ivory phallus to the tightly puckered rosebud of her anus.

Screams began to deafen both of the men as she cried, "No! No, please! No! Stop it! Why?" as the mushroom head of the phallus penetrated into her reluctant, forbidden entrance. It wasn't too thick; certainly not as thick as either he or Draevan was, but that didn't matter to her. She was positively beside herself.

"It hurts!" she whimpered, wiggling her bottom from side to side as much as she was allowed to. "It hurts! It burns! Please, Taric, sto-ho-hop!"

Although it was oiled, her bottom was tight enough that it was giving the phallus a lot of resistance as Taric pushed it into her. Her opening widened to take on the girth. It was horribly erotic to watch, although she was whimpering like a wounded puppy now. Despite her whining and discomfort, her body was responding to the intrusion merely by moistening her hairless pussy lips. Her body was begging to be taken, and the smell of her sex was making his mouth water.

She emitted a sob as the knot at the end of the phallus, thicker than the rest of it, pushed into her until it stopped at the hilt. "It hurts," she moaned.

"*There's only so much more I can take before I lose all control,*" Draevan warned, passing Taric his belt. "*Get it over with.*"

"Kyra," Taric said, standing back to his feet and doubling the belt over in his hands. "You were a very bad girl, weren't you?"

Kyra's shoulders shook as she continued to cry.

"Kyra."

She sniffled and nodded. "Yes," she whispered.

"You ran away from us. Twice. You betrayed our trust. Twice. We had to save your life. *Twice*," he felt more exasperated with her after every word. Damn it all, she hadn't even needed to have spent the last month in the dungeons! Draevan and Taric would have happily protected her from that!

She nodded more.

"And what do we do with our naughty wife?" he asked her.

She didn't answer until he repeated the question again, and then she whispered, "Um... They... You..." She swallowed.

Draevan cut in. "We punish their naughty bottoms inside and out, don't we?" When he said that, he saw that even the back of her neck blushed in response. She was ashamed, and her shame was delicious.

"Please don't spank me," she pleaded. "I can't take it! I can't! Take this—this *thing*—out! I beg you!"

"Why would you want that? It's making this pretty little pussy of yours sopping wet," Taric told her huskily, guiding his fingers over her plump, damp lips there. "You know what that means, Kyra?"

She gave another whining moan, but shook her head.

"It means that your body wants this. It's getting itself ready to take a man's cock." She shuddered from the effect of his words. "Now stay still and try not to clench. This won't hurt as much if you learn to relax your bottom."

"Eeek!" she cried, wiggling her bottom about before the leather belt even landed on her skin. She certainly wasn't relaxed. He had a completely different style from Draevan, who delivered his punishments slowly and methodically. Taric, however, landed several slaps of the belt against her in a flurry, and then he let her catch her breath before he landed another five.

Her bottom was now dashed with welts, and her scream was so loud her voice had broken. Her body was trembling. "I'll be good, I'll be good if you stop! I'm so sorry!" she murmured pitifully.

He stopped to run a finger across one of the welts, but then when he glanced away he noticed that Draevan had let go of her hands and was now talking gently to her. "You are our most glorious possession," he told her softly. "Don't scare us to death by risking your life. You don't yet understand how important you are. You're irreplaceable, Kyra. "

Her lip trembled in reply before fresh tears squeezed from her eyes. "I'm sorry," she told him, her voice hoarse.

"Me, too," Draevan told her, then stood up, his expression all business. "On your knees."

She made a show of slowly pulling herself to her knees and moved her bottom away from Taric, giving him a betrayed expression, but when she looked back at Draevan, she nearly fell backwards on the bed. Draevan was unbuttoning his breeches before her, and how she hadn't seen it coming, Taric couldn't guess.

Taric could be well-described as a voyeur. Certainly, he liked having acts performed on him, but there was also an inherent satisfaction of watching women try to please Draevan. This worked well because Draevan, since they were teenagers, was so big-headed he claimed he performed better with an audience.

The view this time was picture-perfect because their wife, even though she wasn't innocent, was at least virginal, and the girl still seemed to be trying to hold the scraps of what was left of her pride together.

She was going about that all wrong. Their own personal desires in bed wouldn't support a girl with stern pride; they needed a submissive slut, and they simply weren't above creating one from scratch. It was part of the plan—one they had spent a long time hatching up with each other as they searched the forest for Kyra.

Pride was for *outside* the bedroom, hopefully reserved for her role as wife and eventually mother, and the sooner she realized that, the better things were going to be.

As Kyra jerked her body back, Draevan grabbed her wrist and stuck it boldly into his breeches. From her expression, one might think he just made her stick her hand into a snake pit.

Taric barely held back a laugh as he thought that, in a matter of speaking, that's exactly what Draevan had done.

"Feel that?" Draevan asked her huskily, his hand continuing to keep hers gripped to his cock. After she tried more violently to pull her hand away, he gritted his teeth, "Keep it there, darling, because your job is to pleasure it. You'll be pleasuring it with your pussy, mouth, and ass before you know it, but we'll start with your hands. I'd get used to it if I were you."

"No," she hissed, and tried to grab her hand back once again.

Draevan grumbled and let her go. "Taric, she needs another fifteen," he suggested, waving at her.

Her hands flew back behind her bottom. "No, no, no!" she pleaded, but Taric obliged Draevan, kneeling up on the bed and grabbing ahold around her and raked out fifteen more stripes against her bottom.

Her bottom rocked side to side during the quick onslaught, and the fifteen came down upon her so quickly she didn't quite have time to breathe until it was all over.

"I hate you both!" she sniffled. "You can't make me do this. I'm an elf, don't you understand? I'm too good for this!" Well, at least she didn't mince words!

Taric raised an eyebrow at Draevan and then reminded her that they could indeed make her do this, and that the life they offered her was far better than what was ever offered to her by her kindred. "You might be an elf," he added, "but you're *ours* first! You have duties!"

"No," she cried in protest, shaking her head.

"Taric?" he said, waving to her bottom, which was already as red as a cherry.

She hustled to her knees again, only now she grasped her hands toward Draevan and clumsily opened the last button of his breeches, which sprang his entire length free from its confines.

Her shoulders slumped when she saw with her eyes what she was going to be dealing with for the rest of her life—it was surely larger than she'd hoped. After a moment, however, she reached forward and, with hesitation like she might have if forced to pet a scorpion, wrapped her delicate fingers around it.

"Mercy," Draevan rasped, then looked up at the ceiling as if he was suddenly drunk with pleasure. He grabbed a fistful of hair roughly, but then dragged his thumb across her temple in an attempt to pet her. "Good girl."

When he did that, Taric noticed that her nipples tightened to tiny pink pearls. Interesting—she was getting aroused even more by that treatment. He lowered himself behind her, wanting to discover if his hypothesis was correct.

Draevan was guiding her hand across his length to teach her how he liked to be stroked, and Taric moved his large hands around to her front, stretching his fingers across the belly that would soon carry his seed. "You like touching his cock, don't you?" he rasped in her ear, reaching up to boldly close his fingers across ones of her puckered pebbles. "You were a bad girl, weren't you? But now you can be our naughty little slut..." he sucked one of her earlobes into his mouth and nibbled on it. "Later you can be our good little wife. Now, don't you feel empty, like you're missing something? Wouldn't it feel good being filled with our flesh? Soaked with our seed, having it stream down your thighs..."

Hell, the imagery was making *his* mouth water. He

dipped his finger into her pussy, but he didn't have to feel inside of her to find her wetness. Even her inner thighs were beginning to show her desire. "That's it, baby. Daddy knows what his little slut likes, doesn't he? We're gonna take good care of you."

He wouldn't have been so confident, he was sure, if her body wasn't already beginning to ease against his, molding to him like a juicy peach. He brushed against her clitoris and felt her whole body shudder with expectation. He felt his own muscles tense with desire, his mouth salivating from her reaction to him. This was turning out much better than he had anticipated. "Keep stroking him, little one," he growled lustily. "And your husband there would like you to give it a little kiss. Wouldn't you like to make him happy like a good girl? Hmm?" He pinched her nipple, and she panted.

She gave a whimper, leaned forward, and put her face towards Draevan's cock. Draevan hissed out a curse as she hovered her lips over the tip of his cock and then lowered them to it.

"Use your tongue like a good girl, and I'll pull out your plug," Taric promised, and Draevan certainly seemed to welcome the sudden vigor that Kyra unleashed. She wrapped a second hand around his cock, right near the base, and flicked the soft skin with her tongue.

Draevan roughly combed his fingers through the roots of her hair, obviously pleased. Taric continued to sensually move his fingers through her folds, teasing her hard nub there.

"Here," Draevan rasped to her. "Take this into your mouth, and suck." She did, nervously at first, but then with more confidence. Draevan groaned, then ordered gruffly, "Look up at me... That's a good elfling."

Taric kissed her shoulders all the way across, then her neck, moving slowly and laboriously. Eventually, he grabbed at the edge of the bottom plug. "Relax," he cooed to her, then slowly dragged it out of her.

Her body froze, and she stopped sucking. But immediately Draevan hissed, "Not now! Keep going—gods!"

Taric had frozen too; he had suddenly been overcome with a need so rich that he almost came in his trews... He had never done that before; not without touching himself. He had never just come like that... It was startling, and it took him a moment to right himself enough to continue to pull out the plug. "Were you close to coming?" he gently teased her, trying to keep himself from panting. He stopped playing with her until the plug was completely out. "Not yet, little elfling. I want to be inside you when you come."

She moaned around Draevan's cock as soon as the plug was out of her bottom, closing her eyes with happy pleasure. "Don't worry," Taric said in her ear. "That was a little big for your first time, but you'll get used to it."

Her eyes cracked open again, her expression slightly panicked.

"Oh, yes," Taric purred at her, teasing her bottom-hole with the tip of his thumb. "This bottom is ours, elfling. And you'll learn that we own it, and then you'll learn to love it. I promise you." She moaned at his teasing touch again, and Draevan groaned as the vibration of her moans was putting him in a desperate state of bliss.

Taric spread her legs and came behind her. He made quick eye-contact with Draevan. "*She'll never be more ready. I have to take her*," he told Draevan before offering graciously, "*Unless* you *want to be her first?*"

"*I couldn't... stop... if I wanted to...*" Draevan panted.

Taric undid his trews, grasped his length in his hand, and put the smooth head of it to her entrance, slicking it up and down, lubricating his staff with her wet heat. He kissed the small of her back, then reached around with his other hand to continue playing with her. "My pretty little toy," he growled under his breath. He felt her begin to writhe against his fingers before he grabbed her around the waist and pushed the head of his member in. He heard her squeak around Draevan's cock, and when he looked up he could see that Draevan was keeping her mouth on him by grabbing a fistful of her hair.

"Good girl, it's okay now…" Taric cooed as he continued to press into her. He quickly found her barrier and held her slightly tighter with one arm as he gave a firm thrust forward with his hips.

"Armph!" she cried around Draevan's cock. Both men began to pet her consolingly, making shushing noises.

Her body froze again, and a pained look appeared on her face. For a second, Taric feared that he'd hurt her, but then he felt her muscles clench down on him in rapid succession, her hips bucked under his groin.

Suddenly, everything unraveled. Draevan and Taric both roared out curses—they were coming, all three of them, at the same time. He had never even heard of this; it was rare enough for two people to come at the same time, let alone it happening in a threesome.

Not that he was really thinking deeply about the strange occurrence—he felt for a moment like he had turned to mush, and when he came to his senses, he was ashamed.

He hadn't even bottomed out in her; he had only just finished breaking her hymen when they'd come.

He pet the side of her thigh, expecting her to break out into tears at any moment, especially because Draevan had emptied into her mouth, but it never came. Draevan broke the silence by saying, "Alright, love," and gently pushing her away from him lest she cause him pain. She had still been suckling… And she had actually *swallowed* Draevan's seed without any need for Draevan's urging.

Taric cursed himself, slowly pulled out of her, and then lay down on the bed, pulling her up against his chest. "Wait—wait," Draevan said, confused. "You're… Done? Already? Lords, man! You barely just started!"

"I noticed that she wasn't sucking your cock for a substantial amount of time either,

Cousin," Taric replied tersely.

Kyra suddenly reached up and grabbed Draevan's arm, pulling him down with her. He happily embraced her, cuddling her into his arms. "You tasted good," she told him in a tired murmur. "So... good..." She slowly pressed her cheek to Draevan's chest and began to kiss, and then, when he didn't pull away from her, she even nibbled. Her body twitched involuntarily, and she wiggled her hot bottom against Taric's groin, trying to grind her wetness against him, but she made a sound when kissing Draevan that sounded like a low purring.

"Okay, my sexy little elfling, there's time for that later," Draevan told her teasingly, pulling a few strands of her white hair away from her face and securing it behind her ear. "Go to sleep."

"I'm not tired," she said, hunkering her head against Taric's extended arm, but a second after she closed her eyes, the purring sound she made while sleeping was deep enough for Taric to feel the vibration against his chest.

"*She must have enjoyed herself,*" Draevan said. "*Despite your poor performance.*"

Taric's eyes narrowed, and he adjusted his body up so he could look over her head and properly glare at his cousin. "*You're just jealous that you didn't take her maidenhead,*" he told him aloofly.

"*I'm not jealous of shit. Did you see the way she sucked cock? She has the eyes of an angel and the mouth of a tavern wench. By the end I had to pull her off me!*" He grinned proudly, then he shook his head. "*Searching for her the last month has been entirely worth it. I nearly lost my mind when she was scaling down the side of the castle, though,*" he added with a frown.

"I did, too, but—now that danger has passed—I'm proud of her. Even if all the elves looked as good as Kyra, she would still be the best choice. Say something happens to both of us—she has enough savvy to get our children somewhere safe. And we have to think about this, Draevan, because if you think the Dark Wizard hasn't heard about us killing the giant yet, he will soon enough. He's not deaf, blind, or stupid. If he hasn't heard of the prophecy yet, it doesn't mean he never will. And when he does, he might try to do something about it. We have to keep her safe until our sons come of age."

"*The prophecy is made. Our son will kill him. You can't change fate,*" Draevan said, shaking his head.

"*Yet we were frightened enough about Kyra when she was a slip away from plummeting to her death,*" he reminded. "There's always a chance, Draevan, that things won't fall into place like we hope, and the Dark Wizard is not going to just sit in the North and wait for the Chosen One to come and lop his head off," Taric reminded. "This has to be played perfectly. Remember, there's nothing that says that any of us survive very far as soon as we get her with child. From here on out, we really don't know what the future will hold. Not really. Hell, there's no true guarantee that any of us are involved in the prophecy. I'm still not fully convinced, myself."

"When are you convinced of anything?" Draevan grumbled and petted his fingers through Kyra's hair. Taric rumbled, "*The elves don't seem to know the prophesies, and she doesn't know it. I don't see any reason to burden her with that sort of information. Despite that, the plan remains the same. We have to get her with-child… A whole brood, if we can manage it.*"

"*I,*" Draevan said slyly, "*can manage it. You? That's another story.*"

"*Don't be an ass, Draevan,*" Taric grumbled with an eye roll. "This won't happen again. It was so odd—I seriously didn't think I was so close, and then she came, and—"

Draevan nodded. "*Strangely, same for me. I knew I was close, you know, it felt terrific… But I had no idea I was that… close…*" Draevan's words drifted off.

A revelation had come to both of them…

"*You don't think…*" Draevan drawled. "*You don't think that the binding ceremony… that it's… magic, do you? Like it would bind us in that way?*"

Taric shook his head firmly. "*No, that's the most ridiculous thing I've ever heard.*"

"*Why?*" Draevan asked, narrowing his eyes. "*Ever hear of a simultaneous three-way orgasm? I haven't. I wouldn't have even *believed it had I not been there. Besides, you have to admit, when she had stopped in her tracks on scaling down the side of the castle, we were suddenly both worried for her at the same time."*

"*Coincidence, Draevan, is one thing you have no patience for,*" Taric replied, nuzzling his nose into Kyra's hair.

"*Obviousness, Taric,*" he grouched back, "*is something that you have no patience for.*"

"*I see nothing obvious in this situation,*" Taric replied.

"*Obviously,*" Draevan replied, his tone bitter.

Taric grumbled, and then reopened an eye. "*Fine,*" he groaned. "*I'm sure we'll find time to experiment.*"

CHAPTER FOUR

Between her exhaustion, the softness of the bed underneath her, the warmth of the bodies next to her on either side, and being so satiated, Kyra was certain that she had never slept so well. When she woke up, she was starving yet, physically, she was feeling much better. She felt far less forlorn than she had been before.

If it wasn't for the burning in her bottom, the pain still throbbing within the rim of her anus, or the gentle soreness between her legs, she wouldn't have believed that all that had happened wasn't just a dream.

So much pain, so much humiliation… Yet the zealous way she had been taken afterwards was alarmingly addicting. Towards the end, she hadn't wanted it to stop. Despite the fact that she hated them for what they'd subjected her to, she couldn't stop herself from soaking in their attention. And it wasn't as though she were blind to the good looks of her husbands, nor was she able to ignore how good their touches had felt. The force of her first orgasm was nearly unsettling—for a few minutes she'd completely lost all sense of self. She wasn't a person in that moment; she felt like a well-fucked simple-minded animal who only wanted to curl up somewhere warm and settle in her mate's warmth.

Even pleasuring Draevan with her mouth hadn't been loathsome and disgusting like she thought it'd be. In her invisible state she had heard, and once even seen, a woman giving oral pleasure to a man before, but she thought it must be the most disgusting thing.

But Draevan's skin was actually... well, *tasty*. He tasted sweet, and when she got a small taste of precum seeping out of his little hole, she immediately felt the urge to milk more out of him. It was delicious nectar to her, just like a salty type of honey.

Come to think of it, she remembered salivating when she thought of her husbands' kisses. Kisses also tasted good in their own way, but were less salty and more like wine than honey.

Even now, as she smelt Draevan's breath against her cheek as he slept, her mouth began to water, and she fought the urge to nuzzle her nose across his cheek. Hmmm, possibly it was important she eat soon. Maybe she was so hungry that everything smelt good and seemed satisfying, even sex and kisses.

Leaving the bed was impossible, however. She was well-trapped between them; she couldn't get up without waking one or both of them. She would have to wait.

She watched Draevan's chest rise and fall as he slept and the way his eyes rapidly moved under his lids. After a moment, she found herself staring at his lips. Surely, his kisses wouldn't feel so good today? She was less tired and more in her right mind after all...

She stretched her leg over Draevan's and slowly arched her neck to work her way up to his parted lips. She thought he was still sleeping until the next moment, when he put his large, rough hand upon her breast, and kissed her back deeply, kneading her flesh in a soft, pulsing grip.

Yep, he was definitely scrumptious. He looked over her head, and then slowly pulled her off of Taric's arm as he slept, positioning her body under his own body, supporting himself with an elbow on each side of her face. Slowly, he spread her naked legs apart until he found himself half-kneeling, half lying between them. He returned to kissing her—not just on the lips, but all along her neck and her shoulders.

Lord, this was wrong. This was *so* wrong; her bottom had been so punished hours ago that the soft sheets pained her as they rubbed across the skin, grating her like sandpaper. She shouldn't have forgiven them for that, but when Draevan had told her how important she was—not just to them, but the world—it had softened her to them both, even though she had been cursing their names to the high-heavens before that.

She never thought she would ever get married and bear children. She was too ugly, after all… But perhaps that was all a matter of perspective. Most elves found humans unattractive, but she had spent so little time with her own kind (besides her brothers, who were honestly as human-like as she was), that she could look at Draevan or Taric and see them for the handsome humans they were. They were strong, powerful. They were smart enough and quick enough to catch her in the first place, and for lamb's sake—they were *giant killers*!

Draevan parted her knees even more, and she felt him put his thickness against her sore, moist entrance. She hitched a breath. He was so large… that's one of the only things she had been thinking when she was suckling him; how it almost didn't fit in her mouth. And, if that was the case, how was it ever going to fit inside of her *body*?

"Wrap your arms around my neck," Draevan whispered to her softly, driving her mad by rubbing the soft head against her swollen clitoris. "I'm not going to hurt you, Kyra. Trust me."

He must have noticed worry and apprehension on her face. She took a deep breath and, not finding another way around it, slowly looped her arms around his neck.

He flicked his member across her entrance and then

slowly guided its head inside of her. She could feel every groove and every vein of his overwhelming thickness. It wasn't too deep inside before he put his elbows back by her head and thrust his hips into her. At first, it didn't slide in so easily, and a focused expression appeared on his face, as if putting his length entirely inside of her tight sheath was a challenge he would successfully attempt come hell or high water.

It pinched and burned as he navigated through the sensitive area, and she forgot to stifle her whimper. He paused and readjusted, spreading her thighs further apart to ease the pain of his entry. For a very long moment, he stilled inside of her and let her accommodate to his thickness. He brought his lips down to the ultra-sensitive point on her ear and then kissed and nibbled down the rim of it, until he was sucking on her earlobe. "Is it beginning to feel good?" he asked her huskily. It was as if he knew, for a certainty, that her answer would be affirmative.

His voice was still quiet, as if he didn't want to wake Taric. She looked over and saw that Taric had rolled over onto his back, but he was still sleeping and even snoring slightly. It felt somehow naughty to have sex with Draevan without Taric at least watching on with approval…

"Look at me," he directed. "I want to see those beautiful eyes of yours." She shifted her glance back up at him. He growled in the back of his throat, and his hips started their thrusts again. "You know what you need, my little slut? A-good-solid-fuck-ing."

She gasped as he thrust hard into her. He was so deep already, so thick.

She felt her chest tightening and her breath hitched. "Don't," he said, suddenly catching her chin with his fingers. "Listen to me right now—don't you come, or I'll spank your ass for you, slut. That's an order."

Her face flushed. "I'm not a slut," she hissed at him. She remembered Taric calling her that before as well, and she was too lust-drunk to argue. He could have called her anything, and it would have made her purr.

He didn't stop thrusting, and his words ground out, "You're one in the making. All ours... Our little elf-slut. Soon you're going to crave our cock, wife. You're going to need it like food, water, and air," he promised her. He groaned, "You're so fucking tight..." He groaned again and lowered his head to her ear again. "Do you feel that? I'm all the way inside of you. Doesn't it feel good? Doesn't it feel right?" He pressed forward, growling like a beast. "You were born for this. You were born to take my cock, just like you're doing now..."

She stifled a shudder; it felt so good that every nerve was on fire. She pressed her lips closed, stubborn. She didn't want to please him by saying something he wanted to hear when he was being so rough-worded.

He nibbled her bottom lip and then pulled nearly his entire length from her; she was worrying that it was ending so soon, but then he just rammed it right back into her. She cried out and sank her nails into his shoulders. Gods, it felt like it was hitting her womb!

"You are so sexy when you cry out," he told her before he did it again. After she moaned in pleasure, he said, "You can tell me how much you like being my little slut. Go ahead, wife. Say it."

She wasn't planning on it, but as he thrust into her over and over again, she began to feel more and more lust-drunk. She was losing control. "Yeah... Yes..." she panted inanely. She felt herself build up to orgasm; she felt it, and she was driven to get there. But it was as if he knew, and he was punishing her for not playing his game. He slowed to a halt. "No!" she growled, gritting her teeth.

"Tell me you like being my little slut, sweet, and I'll let you come," he told her patiently, a grin appearing on his lips.

"I hate you," she growled, and tried to grind her hips on him, attempting to imitate his thrusts in a mirror-image of his own past movements. She was sure it was coming off as desperate, because his grin widened. She bit her lip and then growled, "I like being your..." She swallowed.

"My little slut," he drawled.

"Your... Your little slut," she stammered out.

Finally, he pushed himself back into her. It felt wonderful. Her eyes rolled back with pleasure and fulfillment as his thrusts were once again hard and steady. "That your breasts are mine," he growled as he grabbed one of her breasts, and she knew he was playing a game with her, one she couldn't ignore. His movements felt too perfect.

"My breasts are yours," she repeated, then gasped when he squeezed her hot, welted bottom.

"Your ass is mine."

"My ass... is yours..."

"Your pussy is mine."

"All yours," she assured.

"You're all mine, all of Taric's. We'll share you between us—any way we please."

"Yes, yes—gods!" she whimpered. He seemed to temper himself in a way that made her ride along the edge of passion without letting her fall in. "More!"

"I'm going to put a baby in you, elfling. That's what I'm going to do," he promised, his beastly growling nearly making it sound like a threat. Somehow, the idea was even more erotic. She didn't know why, but somehow the thought of getting pregnant from this tryst made her insane with lust. Draevan began to fuck her harder and faster; her breasts bounced violently with every thrust, her pussy felt sore even as she was taking him in, yet she could feel herself finally get there. "Draevan!"

"Come for me," he ordered her, and surprisingly, she did. His fists bunched the bedspread by her head, and he winced and then groaned. He looked nearly in pain as her muscles clenched violently down on his cock; and in response his cock pulsed, feeling like it was expanding and retracting inside of her. She could actually *feel* his hot cum flowing into her womb, and it felt wonderful. A strange and new satisfaction saturated her entire body.

She panted, but she didn't feel as tired as Draevan suddenly looked. He rolled off of her.

"Wrong side," Taric groaned, sounding disgusted to be touched by another naked man, but in a way that made it seem like Draevan had done that in the past—rolled over on him.

Draevan grunted with surprise and then rolled back to the other side of her.

"Do you share women often?" she asked, rolling unto her tummy and getting up on her elbows.

Taric smirked and shifted his body to his side, "I suppose, yes. There are the rare times when one of us isn't in the mood, but... We share more often than not." He looked over at Draevan. "You were wrong, by the way," he told him.

Draevan grumbled with displeasure.

She raised an eyebrow. "What's he wrong about?"

"He thought that with the binding ceremony, it causes us all to have simultaneous orgasms—if one goes, so does the rest."

She began to giggle. Were they really that clueless? "You have to be *touching me*, Dummies!" she couldn't help but tease. She picked up her pillow and tossed it at Taric's head.

When he pulled it off, he looked over at her with amazement. "Where did you learn that?"

"I'm an elf; I know. There are fairy stories about it. Like the man who masturbated so often without his wife that she left him for a Winter God?" With the blank expression she was met with, even by Draevan, she realized quickly that it wasn't told to human children. "Fine, fine. What about the man who was able to have sex with all fifty of his wives all at the same time?" Still, vacant expressions.

She frowned. "Oh. Hmm... How about—?"

"Kyra? You need to check with us before telling any stories to our future children," Draevan ordered, looking quite serious and shocked at the same time. He turned to look at Taric. "So, I'm at least half right. There's magic involved somewhat."

"I think an investigation still needs to be held," Taric replied, his tone full of doubt, as he kissed her shoulder.

This 'investigation' was sure to include her... their wife, their *whore*. She couldn't get it through her head yet—in twenty-four hours, she had gone from sure death at the end of a rope to being bred by two powerful human giant-killers.

Taric then pushed himself up and climbed out of bed. He immediately went to the door and demanded food be brought in for them. She grinned excitedly. Her hero! "How'd you know I was hungry?" she teased, sitting up.

He shrugged dismissively. "You need to eat whether you're hungry or not. You have your health to see to—healthy women breed better than waifs," he educated, walking to a bowl and filling it up with water. He immediately splashed some across the back of his neck.

She opened her mouth to protest, but then closed it when she had a thought.

Sure, she didn't particularly like her being thought of as a womb with legs. On the other hand, however, from what she could see they had gone through a lot of trouble for her womb alone, and they seemed prepared to go through a whole lot more. Yesterday, it was a pardon, a bath, and a feather-bed. Today, it would be a feast... What would they provide for her tomorrow?

She wondered if their thinking they could breed her might just be the best thing for them to think.

Besides, no matter how kindly or warmly they acted towards her, apparently they were obliged to give her plenty of pain and humiliation if they decided that she required it...

She blinked and felt her chin drop. *'I must actually be*

what they say,' she thought to herself as she found herself thinking of their kindness as her due. *'Only a whore would allow this rather than offing herself. Lord, not only did I allow it... I enjoyed it.'*

"Hey now—our little elfling is perfectly healthy from what I can tell. Look at her; look at these hips," he gave her bottom a solid spank, and Kyra chirped with displeasure. Draevan merely continued, "These *breasts*!" Draevan unsurprisingly illustrated his argument by palming one of her breasts roughly with his hands. "Gods, she makes me crazy! I'm already up for giving her a re-fill."

She pouted at his crudeness and shrunk away from him towards the far end of the bed. "I'm sore," she complained, drawing her thighs tightly together.

"Besides, I'm next," Taric told him firmly. "We have to always seed her in the same day—remember?"

She blinked very quickly. "What?" They were certainly referring to a discussion made outside of her presence!

"When you give birth, we want to make sure we don't know who the father is. Every child you have will be regarded as both of ours," Taric informed her, gesturing to Draevan and himself. "That's the only way to share a wife—this is how the arrangement is done in the North."

That didn't sound promising. She had a feeling she was going to get a lot sorer. Her husbands were insatiable—they planned to take her often, and they both wanted a 'turn' every day. "It will become easier as we go on," Draevan assured her, reaching over to give the inside of her thigh a consoling pat. "Eventually we'll just forget who had you when."

"Oh, good..." she said, a nervous squeak in her voice.

Although for a hazy, lust-filled moment when Draevan was growling filth into her ear as he rutted over her that morning, she had for a moment fantasized about having a child... Which was surely madness! Besides its impossibility, she'd never seen anyone handle a child. She had no idea how such an idea could have, even for a moment, been so intriguing. "I think we made our little wife nervous, Taric." He brought her hand up to his lips and kissed it gently. "Don't worry, my pet. You'll get used to this arrangement. Until then, just remember that if you're a good girl, you'll think yourself the most spoiled wife anywhere."

"So I'm a well-paid whore," she simplified, narrowing her eyes.

"No," Taric quickly quelled. "You're our wife—*we're married*."

"Right. Whores are paid what they're owed, wives are given what they desire," Draevan casually reworded. "That, and you're ours exclusively."

"Exclusively," she repeated wearily, never having heard the word before.

"You will cause pleasure to us and to us alone," Taric educated, patting her knee.

She knew that was expected of marriage, of course, but the demand still struck her as unfair, since she had no choice in it. "Well," she huffed, knowing that when she pointed out the reverse she'd get nothing but complaints. "Then you'll have me and me alone!"

"Absolutely," Draevan replied easily.

"Of course, pet," Taric agreed.

She frowned; their compliance was quite unexpected. Normally soldiers like Draevan and Taric were too wild to settle down with only one woman. "Really?" she found herself asking, confused. It was certainly strange to have a man call her a slut at one moment and then swear life-long devotion in the next.

The men laughed and Taric grabbed her arm and dragged her over to him. As soon as she was next to him, he picked her whole body up and set her on his lap. She felt his cock harden under her, moving against her flesh, but all he did was affectionately kiss her ear point and say, "You're the cutest thing," he told her, and gave her an affectionate squeeze. "Even though you're obviously a little upset at something. My suggestion is we put some food into you; then you'll be in a better mood."

She doubted that anyone could have possibly handled all that had happened to her in the last month any better, even if on a full stomach, but apparently her doubtful look didn't get that across to either of her husbands. But she didn't have to agree to the food being brought to her as they both set to the task of pestering the nearest servant for aid in feeding their wife.

She was certain when they turned back in her direction that Taric would take it upon himself to get between her thighs and take what was rightfully his once again, but it didn't seem to cross his mind. In fact, the two men dressed and spoke of ordering a dress to be sent up to her.

She blinked. "A dress?" she asked, incredulous when Draevan, who made the order, turned away from the door.

"Well, yes," Draevan said, his eyes shifting as if he worried for a moment that he had done something wrong. "We don't want any servants seeing you in your just your skin. That sight is for our eyes only." He pulled his tunic over his head, flexing his roping muscles as he did so.

She quieted, finding that she didn't really want them to know that she had never worn a dress before. She had spent her life pretending that she didn't like them, mostly because she knew she would never get to buy one. Her family was too poor to buy clothes; what they had was what was worn by the idiots who had tried to fight the giant and had failed, and to date, no female had ever tried the feat. Thus, it hadn't seemed like the garment was in her future.

"Damn," Draevan swore to himself, looking about. "Now I can't seem to find my belt..."

She rolled her eyes and lifted up a pillow, exposing the strip of leather under it like it was a snake lying in wait. "If you can't keep track of it, then you should keep it in your pant loops," she scolded, trying to hide her embarrassment of being so soundly spanked the night before.

Draevan gave a slight chuckle, then walked over and leaned over the bed to grab it. He pulled her long hair back from her shoulder just so he could nip her there with his white teeth.

"She's got more color to her today," Taric said, pausing to stare at her when Draevan was finally looping his belt back around his waist.

"All women get a little color to their cheeks after a morning with me," Draevan replied to him with a shrug and a playful grin.

"Yes, well I did hear laughing's good for one's health," she heard herself quip.

Upon Draevan's hurt expression, she thought she was in trouble and pulled her knees up to her chest. Taric, however, doubled over and told Draevan, "Did you choose a good one, Cousin! She already knows how to push your buttons, eh?"

She still didn't brave even smiling until Draevan cracked a grin, showing his white teeth and shaking his head. "It begins," Draevan agreed.

She felt herself give a little relaxed sigh. She couldn't help it; she was still slightly afraid of her husbands. One second they were brutes set out to spank her, humiliate her, and call her a slut, and the next they were sweet and ready to laugh.

She felt like she was dancing with a couple of hungry bears.

* * *

"*What do you say, Cousin?*" Draevan asked when they'd put out food for their elfling. The servants had refused, point-blank, to come into the room and serve her. It had been shocking, but their horror, which was like that of someone who had been ordered to serve a giant spider, was so sincere that Draevan and Taric were too stunned to get angry with them.

Poor Kyra looked at the banquet Draevan and Taric carried in from the hallway like they had set out precious jewels before her. It was pretty obvious that if the forest hadn't provided it, then Kyra hadn't ever eaten it, or had only done so rarely.

Taric looked back at Kyra, took in the sight of her eating with both hands, and turned back. "*I say if she keeps eating like that she's going to explode.*"

Draevan lifted his eyebrows as if to say, 'You know what I mean'.

Taric sighed. "*Oh, you mean the strange class-system the elves have and that Kyra seems to be settled impossibly low in the food chain? I don't* agree *with it, if that's what you're getting at, but honestly it's a system that's not going to matter in another year.*"

"*Why do you say that?*" Draevan asked, a wrinkle of confusion appearing on his forehead.

"*Because the entire class of untouchables is being caught and executed—there're barely any left. Our Kyra will soon be all that remains.*"

"*Are you saying all untouchables are thieves and poachers?*" Draevan asked, and Taric nodded with confidence, crossing his arms in front of his chest. "*Well, are they untouchable because they're outlaws, or are they outlaws because they're untouchable?*"

Taric sighed and rubbed at the back of his neck with his palm. "*I'm afraid it's the latter. From what I understand, an elf would never hire an untouchable, never feed one or give one charity. If one uses a higher-born elf's sheets, the sheets must be burnt. If they eat from one's plates, the plate must be destroyed. They're not allowed in schools, they're not allowed in the kingdom. They spend their lives being hunted or avoided. All they've been able to do is eke out an existence.*" He shook his head. "*The poor thing.*"

Draevan nodded, but then his eyes widened with realization. "No..." he argued, putting up a hand. "*It's fate.*"

Taric had to argue with this. If he left it up to Draevan, he'd say everything was fate.

"*Think about it!*" Draevan said, shaking his hand in front of him to silence Taric's bickering. "*Our son won't just be the greatest warrior destined to bring down the Dark Wizard, Taric. It's* her *son that will do that… Even if we died and never got to raise our own son, or had to go into hiding, she could actually make the best of it. She's a survivor, Taric.*" He shook his head and grinned. "*Fate brought us to her.*"

He watched any signs of worry of the future leave Draevan's face just that quickly.

Taric furrowed his brow and shifted his eyes back and forth awkwardly. "*I think you've lost your mind,*" Taric finally admitted.

"*For her, I have,*" Draevan admitted with a grin on his face. Seemingly unconsciously, he rubbed at the tattoo on his wrist that sanctified their marriage to her. "*It's like… It's like there wasn't women until her. There were just whores and wenches, pussy and ass. She'll be the mother of our children, Taric. I can't get over it!*" He suddenly crudely adjusted himself, as he always had done when there was a woman around he wanted to see naked. "*Makes me hard as a rock when I think about it, honestly,*" he grumbled. "*It's hard to explain.*" He tried anyway, using only a single word, "*Primal.*"

Watching Draevan look adoringly at anything besides his war hammer or his sword was certainly a sight to be seen! And the thought of standing there and waiting for Draevan to describe feelings that he'd never felt before sounded painful at best. Taric slapped his cousin on the shoulder and said, "*I'm gonna stop you there before you're spouting poetry.*"

Draevan pursed his lip as if annoyed for a moment and then gave him a playful shove. "*You entertain the missus. I'll make sure we get packed up and provisioned properly for the journey home. I want out of here at first light.*"

Taric shrugged. "*What's the rush? Don't you want to honeymoon with our wife here for a while? We have a pleasant job to do, you know. I'd like to bring her home when she's big enough to fall forwards.*"

Draevan laughed but shook his head. "*Do you really think the elves want us here another day now that they've paid what they owe us?*"

"*Of course not,*" Taric said, showing his palms to the ceiling. "But *pissing them off is half the fun. And it's not like they're going to force us out. Their feelings towards us are one-third admiration, one-third disgust, and one-third fear.*"

"*No,*" Draevan said decisively. "*It's all fun and games, but we know too well what they think of our wife. How long until she gets spat on in front of us? And then what are we prepared to do about it?*"

Taric gave a nod. "*You're right. It's better to leave before something ugly happens.*"

"You're so annoying when you're obviously speaking in another language for the sole purpose of my not understanding you," Kyra noted flippantly from the table as she cut into a slice of bacon. "Would it really be so bad cutting me in on the conversation? Time from time, I'm known to have an opinion or two."

"I believe it!" Taric chimed, grinning at her. "We've decided to leave here at first light tomorrow morning."

She swallowed loudly, then looked up to blink at them with a blank expression on her face. He didn't know what to make of her mood, until she fretted, "Well, they'll… They'll just hang me as soon as you're gone…"

"They probably would," Taric agreed, "but that point is moot. You're coming with us to the Northlands, of course. You're our wife—if we have any say about it, you'll be with us always."

"We should probably get you measured for some clothing," Draevan added. "As much as I hate to cover you up for a second, I don't want any other eyes taking in the sights." He grinned, apparently thinking his possessiveness was rather humorous. "And you can't wear that bathrobe forever," he gestured to the red silk robe she had closely knotted to her body.

"Good luck," she scoffed. "You forget easily who I am

and where you are. There isn't a servant that would stand ten paces from me. I know this from experience. Besides," she shrugged her shoulders, "my old clothes will do."

"Your old clothes were threadbare," Draevan argued, an edge appearing in his tone. "If you think it gets cold here, you're in for quite a shock when we start to head north."

"Well, I can't wait then," she grumbled, propping her elbow up on the table and resting her face against her palm.

"I'll take care of it," Taric promised Draevan, just as there was a knock on the chamber door. Taric straightened his shoulders and walked over to answer it. "You just keep your mind on the provisions and the horses."

A servant of the king, a royal emblem stitched on his silk tunic, was at the door and gave a bow. "My Lords," he greeted. "I come to invite you both to sup with the king this eve in order to honor your visit and your departing."

"How'd you know we were departing?" Taric asked, wincing half his face with confusion.

"Oh," the servant looked very pleased. "Oh, we didn't at all. We just suspected that since... you have your promised bride, you'd soon want to be on your way." In other words, the elves were now very interested in the humans leaving the kingdom now that they were no longer in their debt.

Taric gave a wry grin. "Well, you were correct. Send some clothing up for my wife, and we'd be happy to attend."

The servant shifted his weight from leg to leg.

Taric sighed, and he and Draevan both stepped into the hallway, closed the door behind them, and crossed their arms across their chest. "Kyra is not invited, you're coming around to say," Taric gathered.

"It's complicated," the elf at least had the decency to sound half-way apologetic. "But no. The king hoped you'd come alone."

Draevan knew that not abiding by the king's invitation would be insulting to the king, not to mention that it wouldn't help the politics between elves and humans. Yet still he said, "Well, then we're not coming." Draevan's reply was terse, his eyes darkening.

The servant's shoulders slumped. "My Lord, the king, was afraid you'd say that, and if that was the case, then you may bring your new..." he choked on the word, "wife." The servant swallowed. "Although it's highly irregular..."

Taric turned to Draevan. "*Shall we accept? I hate to say it, but it would be politic to go, and they want us there enough that they're willing to at least pretend to get over their prejudice toward our elfling.*"

Draevan tilted up his chin, seeming to be sizing the servant up, possibly because the longer the servant stood there, the more uncomfortable the servant became. Draevan took his time to answer. "*We should,*" Draevan replied. "*I'm sure the king isn't used to dining in the presence of higher life. Our wife will give birth to a great hero; what has their king done lately?*" With that, he walked off down the hallway, his large body dwarfing all elves in his path.

Taric gave a scathing sort of laugh at their host's expense. Draevan was finding a more and more pompous way to view their bride every moment, it seemed. "We will attend," he told the waif-like man who wavered on his legs. "Send up some clothing for our wife."

"But—" the servant began to complain.

Taric walked back into the room and shut the door, drowning out whatever protest he would just ignore anyway. The elves, although they seemed to revere death, lacked any skill to bring it about. They weren't strong, and their bodies were very like children's, even the males. Their bones were more akin to a bird's than like their own. They were easily intimidated and easily passed over.

When he walked into the room, he didn't see Kyra right away. She wasn't sitting at the table. For a moment, he thought she had gone invisible again and swore, turning to look for her in the adjoining room.

It wasn't until then that he noticed a girl sitting on a sculptured bust near the doorway, where a torch would have been lit if it was nighttime. She didn't look like a person; she looked more like a cat or a hawk.

It wasn't Kyra; it couldn't be. The girl looked so different. Her hair was just as long, perhaps, but it was coal black and her eyes were a light sky blue. Her nails weren't glassy and pink like Kyra's were; they were hardly nails at all. They were ivory claws, hooked as if to climb a nearby tree. He looked at her, and she looked at him, but she seemed to be listening more than seeing. "Where's Draevan?" she hissed in a whisper, her voice fearful, her glance skidding to the door into the hall.

Taric stood still and stunned for a long moment, hearing the girl-creature use Kyra's voice, but not believing it for the longest time. "Kyra?" he finally found the voice to say. "What's happened to you?"

"Shh!" She pressed her ear to the wall. "I can't hear anything!"

"We're not under attack! Draevan went to pack, that's all! We were invited to supper!" he exclaimed, his heart thudding from her reaction. "What's happened to you?" he demanded once again.

She turned her head and blinked at him. "I smelled fear," she explained.

Kyra smelled fear? She could *smell* fear? Taric was absolutely astounded, and at the same time, he found that he was slightly embarrassed that anything could have put her on high alert when he or Draevan was around. "That's the king's servant! All the servants practically piss themselves when we're nearby!" he explained. He walked up to the bust and stretched out his arms. "Come down now and relax yourself. Neither Draevan nor I would ever let anything happen to you."

She swallowed and began to slowly climb down.

He finally understood why she looked so different...

Because she was performing magic. "This is what you look like when you're invisible, isn't it?" he asked her as she slid into his arms. He floated her easily back to the ground and wrapped his fingers around her palm. As he was looking at her hand, her nails returned to normal. By the time he looked at her face, gold eyes were already looking back at him.

She nodded. "It's been awhile since anybody's been able to see me like that," she admitted, a slight pink hue spreading across her cheeks. "I'm sorry... I overreacted. I don't feel comfortable surrounded by all this. Everything's off—sights, smells, sounds..." She gestured to the walls with her free hand, an unsettled look on her face.

Suddenly she froze, looking highly disturbed. Her eyebrows twisted upwards. "Did you say that we were invited to supper by the king's servant?"

He nodded.

"So... We'll be eating with *the king*?" she clarified.

"Yes," he admitted. "But don't—" she was already weaving on her feet, her face blanching of all color. "Kyra, *breathe*," he demanded, taking her shoulders in both of his hands and giving her a shake. "Just breathe; you're okay. Here," he pulled the chair at the dinner table back out and pushed her into the seat, then crouched down in front of her. "This is no problem; we'll go there, politely talk about the weather, and leave this place forever," he soothed, petting his thumb across her knuckles.

Finally, she took a deep breath. "I can't go. I can't! You don't understand! I am too far beneath the king's notice, except to execute at his pleasure! I am not fit to handle the man's chamber pot!"

Taric didn't waste any time wondering if he had ever heard something more ridiculous. "Stop talking that way, Kyra. The king is a silly, ridiculous man, and I don't want you to pay him any heed. It's him that's not worthy of your company. Not the other way 'round." He patted her knee through the robe's thin fabric and gave her a squeeze there.

Her eyes narrowed, as if hurt. She turned away. "Not even *you* think that."

He was surprised that she was able to make an accusation out of this! "What do you mean?" he demanded. "You're the most important woman in the universe to me; if you don't learn anything else in life, learn that."

"You call me a whore every chance you get," she reminded peevishly, standing up.

He pulled her back to her seat. "When?" he demanded.

"You called me one last night," she replied, thrusting her chin up like she wasn't hurt.

He squinted. "You mean when we were *making love?*" He shook his head. "You *liked* us calling you names," he assured her, his voice firm, his gaze on her dark as he remembered how wet she was then, how being rough-handled was making her practically shudder with desire.

"I did not!" she denied, her lips puckering. Still, a blush was returning to her cheeks, and her breath was picking up. She had to have been remembering it too, and even the thought was arousing to her. She might never admit it, and she didn't have to.

"You do. And believe me; we're willing to do anything to spread those thighs open for us. You will be treated like a queen by everyone else, I promise you that, but *we own you.*" Without realizing it, he had splayed his fingers on her thighs and was pushing them apart as he was speaking to her. She was even trying to clamp them closed, though she wasn't strong enough for him to take any notice at all of her small struggle.

"Stop," she growled at him, just as he was realizing that he was growing with need for her.

There was something about her that made her different than other women he'd had. None of the other women had made him this greedy with lust. Furthermore, he had never fantasized about putting a babe on a woman before he'd met Kyra.

Maybe it was the way her long, silky white hair draped over her shoulders and over the swell of her breasts. Maybe it was the wideness of her sexy, round hips. Maybe it was because of the exoticness of her features, the innocence of her expression, or the aggression that was always hanging in her tone. He wasn't sure what did it, but there was definitely something that brought out the animal hidden deep within him—the one that wanted to put her on all fours and take her from behind so that before long her flat tummy would be round with his child, her skin glowing, her breasts swollen with milk...

"Taric, stop it." He felt himself shoved back by her bare foot on his chest. It wasn't a kick, but it thrust him backwards.

He grabbed the place in his chest where her foot made contact, shocked. "Don't shove me back," he said, incredulous that she would even try. Did she realize that she was his wife? She hadn't pushed back Draevan that morning when he was fucking her raw in the bed next to him.

"Then don't look at me like that!" she demanded, pressing her thighs tightly back together now that he was no longer edging between them.

"Like what?"

"Like that!" she gestured to the look on his face. "I'm not in the mood to do... that... with you."

"If you're not already, then I can get you into the mood to do *that* with me," he told her, but she was already twisting her face with disdain at the idea. "So you'll open your legs for Draevan but not for me," he concluded aloud. He didn't hide the disappointment on his face.

"I don't have a favorite," she replied quickly. "You're both foolish brutes with egos the size of mammoths and manners like monkeys. If you think the king won't throw me out of the dining hall tonight as soon as I step foot in there, you're insane. You're setting me up for an evening of embarrassment."

He felt like he was heading into an argument, which simply made no sense. He'd done nothing wrong! "It's not optional. We're going to go, because not going would be an insult to this kingdom, which has been our host since we've killed the giant. We're not going without you, because we're not ashamed of you, and we want to display that openly. So, if we go, which we are, you're going… which you will." He pronounced his statement by grabbing her knees and pulling them back open. This time, it took more force.

"I said no," she reminded crisply.

His fingers dug into her thigh. "And I said *yes*!" he snapped, and got a slap in the face for his trouble. He growled, stinging not from just the pain of it, but from the humiliation. He never thought he'd have a wife who would dare to strike him, and he had thought that if she had, he would simply strike her back.

Still, even as angry as he was, he couldn't imagine 'striking her back'. Kyra was too delicate, too beautiful, her face too angelic for that sort of treatment. Not to mention the fact that if Draevan returned to a bruise on Kyra's face, Draevan would surely disembowel him. That didn't mean she obviously didn't think he would; she flinched and put her hands over her face to protect herself.

He grabbed her hands and pulled them down. Looking at her firmly in the eyes, he growled, "Don't ever strike me again, do you understand me?"

She looked like she couldn't decide if she should stand her ground or quake in fear.

He didn't wait for her to make her choice. He stood up and grabbed her around the waist, dragging her to the bed. "Taric!" she cried, her legs flailing as her arms tried to pry him off. "No!"

He practically tossed her up on the bed. She turned to run away, but he pushed her shoulders down until she was flat on her back. He reached down and grabbed the silk tie at her robe and pulled it away from the other garment. He grabbed her hands, dragged her to the headboard, and tied her wrists to it. She immediately tested it, trying to pull herself out to no avail. "What are you going to do?" she fretted. A second later, when she realized how exposed she was to him, she added, "Please don't spank me again!"

Her bottom was still pink from the night before except for some redder welts that stripped across her lower bottom and thighs. "I have more things in my arsenal than just spanking, elfling," he assured her, tying off the knot at her wrists. "I'm going to make you *beg* for me to spend myself inside of you, and you are going to beg me to punish you... Because if you don't, I won't let you come."

She bit her lip and tried to escape again. The headboard was high enough that it forced her to kneel rather than lie flat on her stomach. He pulled off his boots and trousers before he knelt behind her. She dropped her bottom to rest on the heels of her feet, but he reached under her and cupped her sex. Even without having to delve into her folds, he could feel the heat of her need.

He clicked his tongue against the roof of his mouth. "You've only been without a cock for three hours, pet, and now look at you." He nipped his teeth on her shoulder, feeling his excitement growing as well. She shuddered when he flicked her clit with his fingers. Her body was so unbelievably responsive to his touch. He could see her body flush already from his attention.

"Stop," she whined, her voice breathy.

He used his knees to shove her thighs further apart. "I haven't even started yet." He kissed down her spine as she continued to whine. He nipped the clef of her ass when he came to it, nuzzling her soft flesh, using his hands to thrust her bottom up. Slowly, he crawled down between her legs, set on tasting her.

"What are you—?" she asked, looking down at him as flipped onto his back and grabbed her thighs. He sucked her bare, pink clit into his mouth, and she cried, "No!"

trying to squirm her thighs and get away from him. "No, stop! It's disgusting."

"You taste like honey, Kyra. It's far from disgusting," he argued lowly before he licked her again, humming happily to himself. He delved his tongue into her moist entrance, loving the taste, loving the sound of the whining and the moaning she was making. "Stop," she said, sounding weaker every time she said it.

He moved his hands from her thighs and gripped her ass with his hands, thrusting his tongue deeper into her.

She gasped. "T-T-Taric!"

She had no idea that in another moment he would start playing with her bottom hole. This time wasn't like last night. He was using his fingers now, and teasing the small, puckered entrance as he continued to lap at her. Using her own juices, he lubricated the entrance and teased a finger into her. She tried to buck away, but his free hand firmly grasped her hip in place. He felt her toes curl against his thigh as he slowly moved the finger into her. "Please, stop!" she begged him. "It hurts."

"Relax, then," was his unsympathetic response. He delved his finger into her until he was knuckle-deep. "Get used to it, sweetheart. This tight little bottom of yours will be pleasuring my cock before you know it."

"No!" she snapped stubbornly, once again trying to jerk her hands free of the bedpost.

He gave her a firm spank. "How much do you want to bet, slut? You're mine." His own eyes widened at that—he had never been this aggressive in bed... ever. Quite the opposite—he had let women tie him to the bedpost before and take control of his body. With Kyra, however, he felt the need to fully possess her, to dominate her, and to have her admit that she loved it.

And she did; she might be whining and mewing angrily at him, but her desire was dripping down her thighs, and as he moved his finger in and out of her bottom, she began to move with him.

She was trying to get herself off, even. She was panting now, and he could feel her muscles begin to clench.

He stopped everything he was doing, pulled his hand away from her, and gave her a punishing slap on the ass again. "No you don't."

"W-W...What?" she asked, her voice sounding dazed.

He moved his body upward until his shoulders were aligned with the headboard and he could feel her silk hand-tie on the back of his neck. His member was right under her slick entrance. "You don't get to come until I allow it. *If* I allow it. You've been a very bad girl, Kyra... Denying your husband, striking him, being impossibly stubborn... Why would I let you have your pleasure?"

Her jaw locked tightly, and her eyes narrowed darkly at him. "I don't even want you to touch me at all!" she lied, turning her head away from him.

Smiling knowingly, he moved his lips to her pink, puckered pearl of a nipple and flicked it with his tongue. Her body was becoming more yielding to his movements, finally relaxing, although she was far from happy. He felt her spread her legs, and her pussy pressed up against his length. If she thought he was going to penetrate her right now, she had another thing coming. At this point, it wouldn't take much, although she wasn't the only one in need.

He was as hard as steel; there was nothing he wanted to do more than bury himself in her and fill her with his seed... Nothing, that is, except for make her beg for it.

She was rubbing herself on his length, now. Slowly at first, as if she didn't even want to admit to herself that she was doing it. Shortly, she began rubbing harder. "Anything you'd like to say?" he prompted.

She squinted meanly at him and stopped her moving. He shrugged slightly, trying to play like he didn't care how long it took, and continued suckling at her breast like a hungry infant.

She threw her head back. "I hate you!" she groaned,

obviously frustrated.

"You're going to hate me a lot more, wife." He kissed her collarbone, satisfied already that she so needed her release. "You're aching, aren't you? Poor thing." It was hard to keep the mockery out of his tone. He was remembering that she didn't want to have sex with him at all about a half an hour ago. He listened to her panting and reached up and felt the muscles in her arm tighten as he continued to nibble at her nipples.

"Yes..." she whispered, and he released her beautiful breast from his mouth. "No!" She continued to make moaning and crying sounds as she pulled back from the headboard with all her strength, reaching with her fingers to untie her binds.

He gave her bottom another firm slap, hard enough that she gasped with pain and shrunk away slightly as he lifted her thigh and moved off the bed. "Where are you going?" she demanded, her eyes an ominous, dark gold like he'd never seen before. "You're not going anywhere!"

"I'm letting you cool down," he lied, because he was really walking over to oil his cock.

"What are you doing?" she grumbled when he'd been away from her for a full minute. Her bottom was squirming back and forth anxiously. She was so frustrated that every word she uttered was a pout. "I hate this! Untie me! My wrists hurt."

"Then stop trying to get out of your ties," he advised, and came back to her, his fingers covered in oil. He tucked one arm around her waist and then boldly reached into the crevice of her bottom and exchanged the oil on his fingers with the delicate skin on and around her anus, swirling his fingers, playing with her entrance and finally penetrating it again.

She pressed her forehead onto her tied wrists, looking like she was succumbing to forbear what was coming, surely thinking that he was just going to use his fingers, even when he came up behind her.

He came up behind her and untied her bindings from the headboard. She struggled under him, but he kept her in place until her wrists were tied again and her shoulders were pushed down to the bed. "Keep that ass up," he instructed.

Grumbling under her breath, she raised her bottom up as he pushed himself back to his knees and straddled behind her. He held her shoulders down with one hand as he put his cock at her entrance with the other.

"No!" she screamed as soon as his crown found her tiny, virgin hole. "You can't! You *can't!* Taric, *please!*"

"Shh," Taric cooed, pressing the head of his cock slightly in. "You'll be okay. This will feel good, elfling, just relax."

"You're torturing me!" she cried from the mattress. He noted to himself that she still hadn't begged for him; she was a stubborn little thing.

He pushed his cock farther in. She began to squeak with discomfort, and he slowed so that she could adjust to his girth. She didn't appreciate him being in there at all, screaming, "Take it out! Take it out!"

He had done this with many a more experienced woman and hadn't gotten anywhere near this response… Though he had never been inside of a bottom this tight, either! It felt like a vise was around his cock. He groaned and pushed his hips further against her. "Good girl," he cooed to her, all the anger from before washing away when he heard her voice break.

"It hurts," she whined miserably.

"Give it a moment," he told her patiently, wincing as the tightness didn't seem to ebb. He rubbed his hand across her lower back. He finally inched his manhood all the way into her. He could feel his tight balls hit her moist heat.

Finally, he began to shift in and out of her. Eventually, her muscles started to relax, and his shifting graduated to thrusting.

"Oh!" she chirped, clenching the sheets. He could feel she was close and stopped exactly where he was. He rolled his eyes up towards the ceiling. Gods above, he wanted to continue. He needed his release, too.

"Taric, don't..."

"Don't stop?" he continued for her, a cocky smirk bringing up the corner of his mouth. He rubbed his hand across her back. "Is it feeling good, then?"

She didn't answer, just tried to thrust her hips back against him. He held her tight. "Tell me," he demanded. "Tell me how much my little wife-slut loves the feeling of her husband's cock up her little bottom. Say it."

She whined in response—a long, loud, "Nooo..."

He gave her bottom a sound slap, and she made an angry huff. "Fine," he told her, and when he felt it was safe to continue without coming, he continued to thrust on, taking his time each time he plunged his length into her. It felt amazing. He listened to her whine like a cat in heat, and her moans made him thrust harder until he felt he was at the verge of coming. He came out of her completely and threw his legs over the side of the bed, pinching the base of his cock to keep from coming. He was glistening with sweat, panting hard, and absolutely aching with pain.

"Don't! Don't!" she hissed. "Don't! Go, just go. Just come in me."

He got up from the bed and walked over to clean the oil off of his length, preparing himself to fill her womb and not her ass. He didn't say anything the whole while.

No longer tied to the headboard, she clumsily crawled around and towards him, watching him clean himself off, her eyes wide with incredulousness. "Taric?" her voice was fretting, as if him actually not allowing her to come was beyond cruel. "Please... Please... *Help me.*"

He smiled at this. "I can help you, sweetie. What do you want?"

She huffed, and then he could hear her sob. She was so

angry, so frustrated, that she was crying. He stepped around next to her face and took her chin in his hand, turning her tear-stained face towards him. Her expression, even though it was exactly what he'd wanted, pained him when he saw it. She was flushed, angry, and just plain lost. She was completely out of control of her own body, with no idea what to do about it.

"I need you," she sniffled. "I need you in me. Please, take me. I beg you, please… I need you inside of me." She sniffed again. "However you want, but just—just please don't keep doing this to me. Sp-sp-spank me if you want. I'll never say no again. I just—I just need… I just need you to spend inside of me. I need it, I just… I'm going insane. Punish me, just not like this!"

"You want my seed?" he asked, wondering if his ears had ever heard of anything so erotic. "You want me to take this pussy of yours again?"

"Please, please…" she panted, her whole body squirming. "I'll be… I'll be your slut. I'll be whatever you want me to be. I'm sorry!"

He kissed her cheek, and then climbed back up on the bed with her. He moved his body over her and kissed her mouth. She kissed him back, feeling desperate. "Shh," he finally said, untying her bonds. "Shh, elfling. I'll give you what you need. I just wanted you to know you needed it." He pushed her thighs apart. "Daddy knows what his baby wants," he added suavely, his tone deep. He plunged his cock into her. Her sheath was just as tight as it was the day before, only this time, she was thrusting up to meet his own. "We're training you to be our queen and our slut," he cooed in her ear as he thrust deeply into her. His movements were slow, his thrusts running deep so he could spill into her womb. "Gorgeous, beautiful Kyra. My elfling."

She wrapped her arms around his neck and her legs around his waist as if she was horrified that he might try to pull away from her again. She nipped at the side of his neck. "Give me a baby, Taric," she begged. "*Deeper.* Go deeper. Harder." He felt her nails scratch into his shoulders.

He grabbed his hands around her ass and kneaded her flesh as he rammed himself into her. She had her eyes closed, happily accepting every delicious thrust that he offered. He thought he must have died and gone to heaven. Did she really tell him to make her pregnant?

That was nearly enough to make him spill alone. He wanted to fulfill her, to bring them beyond the edge, though, but his control was wavering. "Come for me, slut. Milk my cock…" At his words, her shoulders thrust back, and he felt her clench her muscles over and over around him.

She began to scream out; he knew it, but he couldn't hear it. He was coming so hard inside of her that he could barely take control of any of his senses—he heard a buzzing in his ear as he pulsed pearl after pearl of seed into her hot sheath.

"Taric…" her voice was suddenly in his ear. He gasped a breath, panting. He realized that he had fallen on her with his weight and forced himself off to her side.

They were now both a sweaty, panting, tired mess—but at least they were satiated. "Don't… Make me do that again…" he panted, putting a hand over his rapidly pulsing heart. After taking a deep breath, he pulled his wife against him, giving her a good swat on her bottom. "Just say *yes*, woman!"

She mumbled something inaudibly, pressed her face against his chest, and then she began to purr.

He chuckled and rolled her to her tummy before he pulled a pillow under her. She woke up just enough to say, "What are you doing?"

"Propping your bottom up," he replied simply, giving her bottom a loving pat. He didn't want his seed dripping out of her, not until it had the chance to take root inside of her.

He pushed himself up from the bed and barely found the strength to put his trousers back on before he made it to the dining table, where he quickly made himself a plate of food. Somehow, he felt like he was starving to death!

He had never fucked that hard before, certainly never with that sort of aggression. She had cried, even, when he entered her bottom, and he hadn't ceased. He had never dominated a woman like that, nor had ever even felt the inclination to.

He looked back at Kyra, whose bare body was still covered with sweat; her arms were thrown up over her head. No wonder Draevan was acting so strange—it was all because of this woman. It was making Draevan into a boyish lover and making Taric into a rough dominator.

Elves were magical creatures, indeed!

CHAPTER FIVE

Kyra curled her toes around the side of the bath, pressing her back against Taric. The warm water was soothing, smelt refreshing, and warmed her to her toes.

"Still hate me?" Taric asked her as he ran a bar of soap across her breasts, making them foam. He'd been doing this for the last five minutes; she was beginning to ponder if massaging her breasts with purpose was the reason he wanted to bathe with her in the first place.

She wasn't sure. She wanted to hate him; she ached to. On the other hand, she realized that she didn't want him to actually go anywhere. She wanted him again.

Well, she wanted him *one day*, after she was through being so sore, which hadn't happened yet. She'd woken from a reverie embarrassed at what she had begged for and aghast at how sore her bottom was now that there was no drunken lust left to ebb the pain.

When she complained, however, he did look like he regretted her pain. He drew her a bath himself and poured her a very tall glass of wine. It was only until she had soaked for a while that he broke down and decided to actually join her in her bath, and then he seemed to enjoy it even more than she did.

"I don't like how long it's taken you to respond," he told her, grabbing the wine bottle off of the floor and pouring more wine into her glass. "Are you too angry to speak to me or are you undecided?"

"Undecided," she replied, tilting up her chin and then taking another drink of wine. She figured she was on half a bottle at this point.

"Well, that's better than angry," Taric said optimistically. "If it makes you feel guilty and in a mood to forgive me further, may I add that *I* would never be angry with *you*."

"You *have* been angry with me!"

"Well, I wouldn't *act* on it," he claimed. She knew by his tone that he was assuring her that he would never strike her. Apparently, her unfortunately handsome husband (for she was certain she wouldn't have any trouble whatsoever hating him if he was ugly and smelled), had a short memory.

"I still have welts that state otherwise, *my dear husband*," she said, turning her head.

"I didn't give you those because I was angry. I gave you those because I don't want you to try climbing out of windows again. In fact, you can accept the idea of running away as a bad one. And I don't know why you only call me 'husband' with either snark or distain in your tone. I am, after all, your husband. I have tattoos to prove it." He pulled up his arm in front of her and showed her the white, paisley design crawling up from his fingernails to his elbow.

"I don't know why you can't understand that most marriages, though apparently not human marriages and especially not Northern human marriages, are consensual. Mine wasn't," she snipped in response. "There's something called courtship here. I mean, I haven't seen much of it, but I've seen enough. I've seen men give their lovers flowers or jewelry or… not strip off their clothing and spank them. That sort of thing." She waved her fingers around dismissively.

"I think flowers are very over-rated. They're everywhere. You'd get ones you liked better if you plucked them yourself," Taric complained, grumbling. When he grumbled, his voice went so low she could feel the vibrations in his chest rattle her spine in this position.

"You're very romantic."

"I *am* romantic, actually!" he defended. "Far more so than Draevan, at least. It was my idea to take your virginity on your wedding night." He shrugged and admitted right after, "Of course, you were unconscious during your wedding night. But the *next* day…"

She made a very skeptical *harrumph* sound.

"Look, damn it, this bath scene is very romantic," he decreed, pointing at the water like she should recognize it for what it was.

"Well, from the uncomfortable *pole* poking into my back, I can assume that this could turn from romantic to you having your way with me at the drop of the hat," she accused peevishly.

He was silent for a moment, only to say, "I have to admit… I like how you referred to my manhood as a *pole*."

Just as she sighed sufferingly at him, their bodies both froze when they heard the door to their chambers open and close. She was close to going invisible again when she heard Draevan's voice say, "According to the servants, you didn't have any trouble having a good time while I was out."

She wanted to sink farther into the bathtub and drown herself. It might have worked had Taric decided not to play the role of her bathing cushion.

"Did we scare them off?" Taric only said, his tone assuring that he was far from caring.

"You must have. They left her clothing at the doorstep," he turned the corner and looked at them. There was a spark of jealousy in his eyes for a moment, and she blushed, but Draevan didn't say anything. He swept down to her face and gently pulled up her chin with his calloused fingers to kiss her on the mouth. When he straightened, he put a small box in her hand.

"What's this?" she asked, looking at the box and giving it a firm shake.

"Luckily, not something made out of glass," he replied with a chuckle. "Open it. It's a gift."

She hadn't gotten any gifts for quite a long time—possibly not since her twelfth birthday, and that was only because her brothers had made an extremely impressive robbery that day.

She untied the silk string tying the little black box together and opened it.

It was a necklace—one made of diamonds. Her heart had absolutely stopped beating, she just knew it. Certainly, she'd stopped breathing as she delicately picked it out of the box.

"Oh, *really*!" Taric huffed in complaint, his voice sounding like he and Draevan were playing a game in which the rules had been most certainly broken.

She rose out of the bath water and, ignoring her own nudity, wrapped her arms around Draevan. He didn't seem to mind that she had made him wet, and he wrapped his brawny arms around her waist and lifted her out of the tub.

"It's beautiful," she told him. Never had she owned anything so fine! She hadn't ever even *stolen* such fineries!

"Not anywhere nearly as beautiful as you are," Draevan assured her, putting her on the ground and urging her to turn around with gentle pushes of his hand. "But I'm glad you like it."

Her hair was already pinned up away from her neck so it wouldn't get wet in the bath, so there was nothing in the way of his lips kissing the nape of her neck as he took the necklace back and fastened it around her throat.

He nipped at her ear, and then brought his hands down across her wet, naked breasts, grabbing them hungrily before turning and grabbing a towel. "And Taric was trying to tell me that *he* was the romantic one," she tattled, smiling up at him as he wrapped the towel around her.

She meant to tease, but Draevan's eyes flashed dangerously in Taric's direction upon the escape of her words. He took a step towards the bathtub, and Taric grabbed the edge as if preparing to pop out of the water and defend himself. Kyra grabbed Draevan's elbow and tugged him in the other direction. "Come on," she urged, leading him into the main chamber. "Show me where these supposed clothes are."

Draevan huffed angrily but allowed her to drag him away from Taric. He poured himself some mead before he sat down in a chair, looking set to watch her try on her clothing. Taric didn't come out of the back room the entire while, and she was sure that was because he was avoiding Draevan.

Draevan looked a little sullen as he sat there, watching her try on dresses like she would have never imagined ever wearing not a few days ago. She could feel his anger surging through him, and it didn't make her feel much better that the anger wasn't directed at her.

He grunted in approval when she donned a white silk robe that highlighted the cleavage at her breasts, and she turned and grinned at him. He didn't return her smile, looking deep in thought, and didn't make any eye contact until she stepped up to him.

She grabbed his mug of mead out of his hands and sat on his lap. He seemed surprised by this display of affection, and really—so was she. Although she wished it was intriguing to see her husbands compete for her favor, she could tell that all it was doing was depressing them— especially Draevan who had been working all day only to be told that while he was working, his cousin was working on *her* and then had attempted, however lightly and jestingly, to claim he was better than Draevan in any way.

He wrapped his arms around her waist and accepted

her kisses, still with a stunned look on his face. "You can be so sweet," she told him, rubbing her nose against his affectionately.

"It's just a bauble," he said, setting his hands on her hips and petting the soft fabric of her new dress.

"I like it that my husband thought enough about me during the day to get me anything at all," she told him, then chewed on her bottom lip slightly.

"Thought about you enough?" he said with a wry laugh, tightening his grip on her hips. "Elfling, I can't get you out of my mind!" He began to kiss her, and she could feel his hard rod even through the layers of clothing, but he didn't try to undress her or anything else. It was as if he would have been happy to kiss her forever.

When she pulled away from him, he frowned with disappointment, but then she slowly braved dropping to her knees before him and tugged at his belt.

"What are you doing?" he asked, as if he couldn't guess. He was suddenly sounding out of breath.

"Appreciating the work you did for us today, husband," she said, knowing that he would love hearing her call him that. Her fingers were clumsy on the leather of his belt. His fingers caught hers.

"You don't have to do that..."

"Draevan," she gave him a firm-lipped smile. "I want to taste you." Based on his raised eyebrow, he looked like he really doubted that. She smirked. "Fine," she said, about to raise back up. "Maybe *Taric* would like to give me something I desire—"

He stood up quickly and put his hands her shoulders, easing her back down to the ground. As soon as she was back down, he rustled quickly to open his trousers.

His rod, if it was at all possible, was even harder than she remembered it being. It popped excitedly up against his lower belly, large, swollen, and red-headed. "Remember," he told her in a heated grumble when she reached up to grab his length, "Be *careful*, you devilish little thing."

She could feel him actually quivering with anticipation, even though she had done it just the night before. She wondered if he would try to aggressively thrust into her mouth, and if he did, how long it would take for him to take over.

"Oh gods, have mercy!" he groaned, and she pulled back, thinking she'd done something wrong when she put his hardened crown into her mouth.

"What?" she fretted.

"Don't stop, woman!" he demanded firmly, grabbing the back of her head and launching her mouth further down his length. Apparently, she had misread him—he was groaning because he was enjoying himself that much. "That's a good girl," he hummed, running his fingers through her hair. "You're so good at this, baby. Suck my cock for me…"

"That's a good girl," he said again, thrusting himself into her mouth with more vigor, his hands on the back of her head. "You know how to drive me crazy. Does my baby love sucking my cock, hmm?"

Draevan did still taste surprisingly good; good enough that she didn't mind him taking control of his thrusts into her mouth. He wasn't hurting her, although she came close to gagging by reflex a couple of times, which caused her eyes to tear. She stuck it out, egged on and encouraged by his moans and compliments, as dirty as they were.

"I'm going to come, elfling," Draevan suddenly warned. "Open wide for Poppa now, because I don't want it to get on your dress." He didn't let her pull her mouth off of the engorged head at the end of his cock; he grabbed her hair and melted her to him.

She felt his bullocks tighten before he even started to grit out a pain-laden moan, followed by his veins pulsing violently against her tongue, all before the creamy heat invaded her mouth. As before, she liked the taste and lapped at him eagerly, swallowing every drop of his seed and then carefully licking her lips clean when he eventually let go of her hair.

He seemed weak in the knees and fell back onto his chair as soon as he tucked his manhood back into his trousers. She used his knees to help herself back to her feet, after which he promptly wrapped his arms around her and pulled her back onto his lap and cradled her tightly to his chest, kissing the top of her ear-point.

She knew she probably should have felt dirty or embarrassed about being so anxious to bring a man to pleasure… But the longer he held her against his body, the more her shame melted away. Draevan was a brute, but he was trying to do good by her. She had a feeling that if something had happened to her, he would be genuinely distraught. She didn't even *try* to get his affection; he was aching to give it to her freely.

The loving moment only ended when Taric stomped into the room, pulling his tunic over his head and sneering at Draevan in their puzzling language.

Whatever was said lit a fuse, because Draevan pulled her gently off of his legs so he could stand up, growling back at Taric.

They rounded about each other, snarling and growling, looking like two dogs fighting over a bone. In the next moment, they were pointing at each other, as if assigning some sort of blame.

She stood there, stupefied by their behavior. She had followed them around for three days in the forest, mostly unbeknownst to them, and she had seen plenty of bickering but never anything like this, nothing that seemed to constitute fighting!

It wasn't long before Draevan shoved Taric threateningly backwards, and Taric came back with a harder shove. She scurried promptly over to them—she didn't want to know how much pain two warriors could deal out to each other. With all the strength in her body, she tried to pry them apart. She barely made them budge , but as they continued to amp up the fight into heavier blows there was suddenly enough space to stand between them. "Stop!" she demanded as loudly as she could.

She was quickly realizing that it didn't even dawn on them that she was there, or at least they figured she could be avoided while they grabbed each other's shirts, snapping at each other. She was getting squished by these hard, violently-moving bodies!

She didn't know how, it all happened so quickly, but an elbow collided with her cheek. She immediately hit the floor, grabbing her face, thinking that something had been broken.

The men stood still, still with each other's shirts grasped in their fists, all anger from them quickly dissolving into horrified worry. At once, suddenly gaining movement, they released each other in the same moment and rushed to her side on the ground. "Gods, Kyra!" Draevan fretted. "I'm so sorry, baby! I didn't mean to! It just slipped..."

Taric was already gently trying to pull her hands from her face. "Come on, let me see, honey..." he urged her softly. Hesitantly, not wanting to release her hand with some unexplainable and unreasonable fear that it would get worse if she didn't protect it, she lowered her hands a little and Taric immediately took her face as if it was made of thin glass and turned it so that he could see her face better.

"Nothing's broken," he assured Draevan. "Let's get her something cold to put on this until supper."

She heard Draevan swear, mostly to himself, as he got up to move around.

Taric's thumb stroked across her better cheek. "Poor thing. I'm sorry about this... This was my fault, too. I shouldn't have said anything..."

"Why were you even fighting?" she snipped.

Taric sighed, picked her up from the floor, and guided her carefully to a seat. "I was jealous because you went to him so willingly, while I felt that I had to try so hard to get your attention. I accused him of trying to buy your affection… He accused me of trying to get you to think of him as some cold, bumbling lout, and one thing led to another…"

She snorted. As she suspected, the cause of the argument seemed so childish. "Me doing things with him doesn't have anything to do with you, Taric," she said, meaning it in the nicest way.

He frowned, a grimace forming on his face. She had never seen someone look so struck and heart-broken. It was simply unfair that he wanted her to actually like him after he'd made it so clear that she was only good for two things: pleasuring him and eventually having babies, only half of which she believed she could ever really do.

She didn't want to tell them and allowed them to have the fantasy, but she still didn't honestly think she *could* have their children. Humans were too different than elves, and there certainly hadn't been a cross-breed before that she'd ever heard about. Chances were that she could have their children as much as a dog could ever have a kitten.

She simply didn't say anything because there were those moments of tenderness she didn't want to miss. She knew human men treated the mother of their children far differently than they'd treat a whore they only wanted for sex… And that's what she'd become. She was so close to being seen that way, already…

Taric grumbled, and Draevan passed him a kerchief full of ice he had just chipped right out of the window—it must have frozen over during the night. Taric carefully pressed the lumpy coldness against her cheek. She took over for his hand, pressing it to herself. He brushed back a loose strand of hair behind her ear, stood up quietly, and walked away, leaving her with Draevan.

"Oh, Kyra…" Draevan breathed, kneeling on the floor to be more level with her. "I'm really—"

"Nah," she grumbled, feeling preoccupied. "I'm fine.

At least I got you to stop fighting."

He snorted. "We're used to bruises," he assured her. "It would have meant nothing to us. We've fought wars, Kyra. We could probably lose a leg and not notice."

She raised her eyebrow at his exaggeration, and he smirked at himself. "We'll be more careful next time," he promised. "We're not used to anyone getting between us."

"I really wish I didn't have to," she said with a sigh.

* * *

"Stop touching it!" Kyra snapped at Draevan when he reached over and petted her long, thick braid once again. He didn't know why he liked doing it; it was just as soft as rabbit fur, and the hair felt good against his fingers. "It's not easy to style now that it's all clean," she pouted, as if being clean was such a troublesome thing. She pulled her hair away protectively, letting it fall over the shoulder farthest from them as they walked.

Draevan grinned mischievously to himself and reached over to offer his arm as they walked.

She smirked, bit her lip, and curled her arm around his bicep, letting him play with her fingers when she did.

He took a breath. Everything was finally right with the world—he and Taric were rich, they killed the giant, wed their elf-wife, and if they were lucky she might be already with child. And there she was—a pretty little petite thing that just sparkled whenever he was the slightest bit nice to her.

The only thing cramping the evening right now was Taric, who wasn't himself. Taric was normally the wide-eyed smart, resourceful one with an open mind. He normally didn't allow himself to get depressed or foul-tempered, but right now he was the spitting image of an ominous thundercloud as he marched behind them, his hands in his pockets, his eyes pursed into a stony glare.

He didn't understand how the man could spend the

afternoon fucking their goddess of a wife to the point that the servants were talking about it and still be in such a rotten mood. He had accused Draevan of trying to buy Kyra's love, but Draevan hadn't meant to. He hadn't thought about trying to get her to like him above Taric at all... The necklace was just shiny, and Draevan had heard that women liked shiny things. He only wanted to make the poor thing happy, since she seemed so awkward and saddened when he'd left that morning.

Taric normally wasn't one to try to spur Draevan's anger, either. Draevan could be a violent man, and Taric knew it. Yet when Taric had come in and boasted in their secret tongue, *'You can enjoy her mouth, Cousin, because I took her tight little ass today until she was begging for it,"* Draevan was overcome with the urge to thump his skull for him. Taric had never said anything of that sort to him before; it was completely out of character.

Draevan wasn't stupid enough to wonder what had made the change in Taric. They were fighting over possession of their own wife. One they were both married to, both lawfully and even magically, and that wasn't going to change.

When they were boys, they'd known they would share a wife and had never thought they would bicker with each other over her. They'd certainly never competed over women or whores, even though Taric would allow himself to like a woman much more than Draevan ever allowed himself to, and despite the gruffness with which Draevan would normally be fucking those same women eventually.

Kyra's fingers were as cold as ice before they made it to the dinner hall. Before they were announced, Draevan nipped the top of her pointy ear. "Don't be nervous," he said into her ear. "It's just an elf-king."

She eyed him and blinked at him until he grinned at her teasingly. "Well, if it makes you feel any better, since you married us, you're actually wealthier than the king."

That made her dark little eyebrows shoot up with

surprise. He felt warmth go back into her hands, and he straightened his shoulders as the king's servant announced them as the "Honored guests of the Giantsbane family."

He was never going to tire of being called *Giantsbane*, even if it was the elves that named them that.

The room was packed full of red-toothed, noble elves, and Kyra began to quickly wilt as they regarded all of them with unkind-yet-interested eyes, particularly towards her. The men stood, including the king, and the women sat. The servant led them to their seats, pulling out the chair in the middle for Kyra. She didn't notice, he hoped, how the servant immediately removed his white gloves from his hands when her back brushed up against the man's knuckle as she sat down and tossed them onto a tray filled with dirty glasses, apparently to be disposed of.

"There were not enough seats for all of the members of the court who wanted to come see you off this evening," the king told them with a laugh, sitting down. "It's as if they fear never seeing another human again!"

Fear wasn't the word Draevan would have used, judging from the crowd. Curiously eager would have been a better word for it. Trying to manage polite smiles, Draevan and Taric sat down, following the king's example, and then there was a rustle as all the other men took suit.

"Your wife certainly looks better now than last I saw her," the king said with a smug grin.

"It's amazing what not being locked in a dungeon can do," Taric was quick to reply back with sarcastic flippancy.

"Not to mention *food*," Draevan seethed. He felt Kyra put her hand over his knee and squeeze it to get his attention and apparently to warn him not to make a deal out of her experiences.

He picked up her hand from her knee, brought it all the way up to his lips, and kissed along the knuckle. She looked pleased by this, and even blushed girlishly, but then when her eyes darted to the side, she pulled her hand back as if he'd bitten her and put it back under the table. When he glanced to see what she'd been looking at, he saw that a few elves across the table were shuddering at the display of affection.

Even the king said, "Uck," but he didn't comment any further. He hung back in his chair as servants served soup. "You can't blame me for not feeding a felon right before we tied her up to the noose," the king told Draevan. "Besides—her kind doesn't need to eat as much as *we* do."

Draevan growled and Kyra squeezed his knee again.

Luckily, the king started making conversation with his queen, and then with the other guests.

Draevan could see Taric, on the other side of Kyra, grab so tightly onto his wineglass that he was surprised it wasn't broken. Taric turned his head at Kyra and said, "Aren't you going to eat, wife?"

She glanced at the other elves sipping on their spoons with their overly-pierced lips and shook her head. "I'm not hungry," she whispered, looking miserable.

"Yes, you are," Taric argued quietly. "You slept through noonday. You've got to be famished, so eat."

Kyra nervously picked up the spoon, glancing at the object nervously.

Suddenly the king snorted with laughter. "Look at her! She doesn't even know how to use a spoon!" Draevan didn't realize the king was noticing them again, but apparently he was still watching Kyra out of the side of his eye.

The whole room began to chortle with laughter, except for the three of them, and Kyra looked like she was set to melt underneath the table. Her skin burned a deep red as she eyed the tablecloth, embarrassed.

Draevan ground his teeth in the king's direction. If he wasn't royalty, he would have busted his face for him already.

"Drink from your bowl," Taric advised her calmly, turning his shoulder to the rest of the company. "You don't have to use these; I should have realized you don't use them. You've never had a reason to."

She put down her spoon and, amongst the laughter, she picked up her bowl with her hands. Draevan and Taric followed suit, until the laughter died slightly. "Our wife could teach lessons in practicality. Her needs are delightfully few," Draevan told the king, putting up his spoon and then putting it down. "It makes it all the better when we spoil her with the wealth of a whole kingdom."

That made the king stop laughing, and he even pursed his lips. "Yes," he said. "Killing the giant has done you well. If you were higher born, you could be a king," he added aloofly.

"If we *wanted* kingship, My Lord, then kings we'd be," Draevan responded, straightening his shoulders. "Who would stop us?"

For a moment, the words sat in the air like the threat they were. There was silence for a while after that, and Kyra sat up straighter in her chair. She was still blushing, but honestly so was Draevan. He wasn't used to attention.

Taric sat back in his seat, his body language relaxed, yet threatening, like a man-eating dragon that was merely digesting his last large meal of village-folk. He looked thoughtfully at Draevan, then at Kyra, not saying a word. The only thing that broke his still movements was when he leaned forward, took Kyra's chin in his hand, and kissed the side of her nose, right where her small bruise ended.

Kyra didn't bite her lip or respond to Taric at all like she had done with Draevan, he noticed. She didn't melt back in his direction. Instead, she turned her knees in Draevan's direction afterwards, as if she didn't want Taric to touch her again.

Draevan frowned, wondering what the devil Taric did to her. If his taking her bottom created this much disdain, then Draevan was thankful indeed that he wasn't the one to have done it. After all, his girth was even thicker than Taric's... She might have never forgiven him.

Supper moved slowly, and making conversation with

the people around them hadn't made it pass any more quickly. Kyra refused to say anything at all to anyone, making sure her eyes stayed on her food at all times.

Her differences in comparison to the other elves had never been so evident. Kyra looked stronger than these people around her, even though she had lost so much weight since they'd met her in the forest. Her skin was pinker, probably because she had been outside all of her life and actually saw the sun, whereas the elven royals' skin was a pale white, nearly translucent; they would look veiny and sickly if it wasn't for their tattoos. Her white hair was even shinier, her eyes a shiny gold instead of a pale yellow.

Despite the fact that she nibbled on everything with her delicate little fingers, somehow she was also more feminine than the other females in the room.

They were beginning to get anxious to leave the chamber by the time dessert was served. It seemed like the elves were layering on all the courses to torture them.

"What will you do now, Giantsbane?" the king asked. "Once you leave us, where will you go?"

"Back to the Northlands," Taric offered in a grunt over his glass of wine.

He snorted. "With the girl," he said, sounding disgusted by the concept.

"Of course, she's our wife."

The king winced. "Yes, yes… But you know you don't have to *keep her* as your wife. You've had your fun with her; I've heard that much from the servants. Now you know what it's like between a she-elf's thighs and to take on some magical ability, which is surely all you could have wanted from this little arrangement, or else you would have chosen a higher-born she-elf to take as wife! Apparently you understand that her kind is less than pleasant." He gestured to the bruise on her face, as if it had to have been there from a punishment she was given. "If you just wanted to toss her down a ravine, or something more interesting than bringing her all the way to the Northlands, certainly the world wouldn't be any worse for wear... Then you could take a better wife for yourselves... From your *own people*, perhaps."

Draevan growled defensively, "That bruise was not given to her in anger."

The king shrugged, not believing him. Draevan could tell by the king's chiding glance that the king thought of himself as very wise. "Very well. My point remains."

"Killing her is far from our plans. We'd happily *die* for Kyra," he declared angrily. "We'll never take another wife."

"Well, what about heirs to inherit your fortune?" the king asked. "You have to think of these things. You surely have to take another wife—a human one—soon."

"Kyra will have our children. We plan to have her withchild well before we arrive back into the Northern Lands."

There was lots of tittering in the room when that was said. The king laughed and said, shaking his head, "You really think she can birth you children? It's never been done before, my friend!"

"It's never been tried, either," Draevan growled.

"Trust me," the king said, waving his hand in front of him. "She is not good for anything but warming your bed, and that will feel quite cold before long. If you think one day you can get her to do what you want, forget it. Her kind cannot be taught anything, not even the ways in bed. They cannot be taught to read, work, or use a fork!"

"My Lord, you are wrong," Taric said calmly, but his hands were gripping the table.

The room gasped. "Wrong?" the king said, looking offended. He pointed a tattooed finger at Kyra. "She is the spawn of a long line of traitors and thieves! If I'm wrong, then it's only because you found out something that we haven't! Bring her back to the Northern Lands, if you will. If she is good for anything, it's for spreading her legs like a proper whore! Obviously you don't mind shar—!"

There was no sound in the room now, not even

gasping. Everyone stood up from their chairs to watch Taric, who suddenly had thrown the king into the wall behind him and had him writhing in a choke-hold. He was being held against the wall so high, that his legs flailed.

Draevan grabbed Kyra's arm, stood up to pull her body behind him, and pulled out his sword, brandishing it before approaching guards. The guards stilled, apparently not wanting to wrangle with a man who'd taken on the giant.

"Say another word to my wife ever again, *Sire*, and I will end you," Taric growled. His body language was unlike anything Draevan had ever seen. It was strong, but uncannily calm. He choked harder, and the king made a gurgling sound. "And if you call my wife a whore again, I will do everything I can to bring down your kingdom, the gods as my witnesses. Do you understand?"

"Urghh..." the king gurgled, doing something that looked like a nod as he turned blue.

Taric released, and the king dropped to the floor. He pulled out his sword from his satchel, eyeing the guards.

"Well, kill them!" the king choked. "Thugs and low-lives!"

The guards looked a little pale at the order and didn't make any aggressive moves. At least they were smart enough to realize that they didn't have much of a chance against such warriors. Draevan held his sword with both hands, looking like he would be pleased to cut off the head of the next elf to make a move or even sneeze. Taric crossed the room to...

...Kyra? Damn, she looked different... She looked paler, with hair as black as night... Claws, even!

Taric pulled her away from the wall behind Draevan, which she was crouching against, looking horrified, and then he pushed her in front of him. "*Go now, and don't give away her location. They know she's the easiest target.*"

"*What do you mean?*" he snapped back.

"*She's gone invisible,*" Taric said. Draevan was sure there was something he didn't understand about what Taric said at first—their language wasn't perfect by any means.

They were rushing out of the door before he finally remembered that she was an elf, and therefore could do magic, like turn invisible. Apparently, she used her skill as soon as she saw serious trouble. "Straight to the horses. Down this way," Draevan instructed, turning down a hallway.

It was too quiet for the aftermath of an attack on the king. The halls were empty, even the stables were empty of attendants. "Where is everyone?" he demanded.

"Invisible," Kyra answered in a hiss, as if his question was stupid.

"You can see them?" Draevan asked hopefully.

"No," she replied. "But they breathe like snoring elephants."

Draevan frowned, not able to hear anything.

"Keep going," Taric suggested, helping Draevan saddle the horses and hook the packed-up satchels and supplies to the back.

Kyra had her own horse, but Draevan hesitated to put her upon the saddle. Instead, he picked her up by her underarms and set her on Taric's then quelled her opening lips with a stern look.

She didn't look like a happy horse-rider, and she looked uncomfortable in the saddle, like a child might. But she was a good girl; she didn't say anything, and she didn't even grump or grumble at them. He tied her horse up to the back of his saddle to direct it with no rider.

They wasted no time with words. Taric and Draevan gave each other a readying glance then climbed upon their horses and took off into the night.

Swii! Swii!

"Fuck!" he brought up his shield, knowing the sound of an arrow whizzing by his ear when he heard it. "Cowards!"

Taric kicked the horse into a fast gallop, "Get into the

woods, hyah!"

"Ah, shit," Kyra was saying, then tried to direct their horses through the thick foliage. "Left! Right! Taric, right! *Right!*"

Taric groaned and obeyed. Since they survived, Draevan followed suit. When he turned his head, he turned his head to the left-path, the one not taken, where an arrow hit the ground and immediately sank.

Draevan gulped. *Quicksand.*

It was suddenly making sense why there were given such specific directions to get out and into the kingdom when they wanted to go hunt for Kyra... The castle wasn't just hidden—it was sitting in the middle of a giant death-trap!

He stayed closer to Taric's horse. "Just do what she says, Cousin!" he shouted. "She'll keep us alive."

"Well, somebody's got to!" he heard her cry ahead of him.

Draevan frowned at first, then smirked as they galloped along, taking directions until they were so deep in the woods he doubted even an elf could find him... He wouldn't know the way back himself. The immediate danger was gone.

He looked around him, just to make sure, and when he turned back, Kyra's body was turned in the saddle. She was back to her beautiful, ivory-haired self, and she was kissing Taric like there was no tomorrow.

He felt jealousy swarm up inside of him again. He grunted. For the first time in his life, he realized that he didn't really want to share her... but that it was better than having nothing at all.

CHAPTER SIX

As they settled into a part of the woods so dark she could barely see, the horse stopped. She took a deep breath, thankful to make it out of the kingdom with nary a scratch.

She was grateful and filled with emotion. For starters, guilt.

Everything that the king could have said about her he'd said, and her husbands stood protectively by her side. Taric had risked much to threaten the king like he had.

At first, she was surprised that the king calling her a whore had been the final straw. After all, they called her a slut in bed all the time... But it made her finally realize something that Taric and Draevan had been probably trying to get across to her, only they were truly brutes who couldn't explain it properly.

In bed, when they called her a whore or a slut, or whatever they said, they didn't mean it. They wanted her to play a part. They wanted her to be sultry and needy and love every move that they made within her, and she did.

It was an act, really, one they liked because it made them feel more like men, more confident in bed.

But when the king had said it... He'd meant it. He

wasn't playing... And that was unacceptable to her men. They would protect her honor and keep it to themselves that she would occasionally act so wanton.

Any anger and confusion she had about them seemed to melt away with that thought. They were brutes holding flowers, her husbands.

As soon as she could, she lifted her legs up, turned back to her visible-form, and turned around in the saddle until her legs overlapped Taric's. Her skirt rode up, but she didn't care. Despite Taric's wide-eyed confusion, she slung her arms around his neck and kissed him hungrily.

Slowly, he returned the embrace, sliding his hands firmly down her waist until he dug his thumbs into her hips. Their kiss was deep, delving, passionate, but he broke it to brush his lips against her ear, saying, "I'm so sorry. I should have listened to you. I shouldn't have made you go to the dinner. You were right."

She smiled and hugged him tighter. "I'm right a lot."

He chuckled, kissed her lips again, and then pulled up her skirts since he had realized by now they were bunched up on her thighs in this position. "I'm in need of you again, honey. You're making me ache." He nibbled on her bottom lip. Her nipples tingled, and her clit pulsed. She wanted him too.

"No you don't!" Draevan huffed behind them. "We're not in a safe location yet, for starters. I see a million little yellow eyes staring at me like I'm a tasty morsel, which would make *her* even tastier. Secondly, you've gotten to take her all day, and you already want her. How do you think *I* feel right now?"

She turned and smiled over at Draevan. "Do you want me to ride with you for a while?" she asked.

"Nah, he wants you to ride *him* a while," Taric corrected with a chuckle.

"I do, but not here and now," Draevan reminded, riding along close to them. He hooked a strong arm around her, and she was sitting in front of his legs before he knew it. The horse whinnied in protest at the extra weight. "If you know this forest well enough to know where the quicksand is, then how'd you get caught by the king's men?" he asked her.

"I was having a bad week," she shrugged. "And finding my kind is the only thing the royal bounty-hunters *do*. They're very good at it."

Draevan kissed the side of her neck. "Well, we're good at killing men like that, and you're good at moving through this devil forest. Just get us through this. Taric—light a torch. I can barely see a bloody thing in this muck!"

Draevan didn't seem to like forests; he was superstitious and spooked easily. If she thought he was prone to nervousness when she was tailing them in the forest over a month ago, that was only because she didn't realize the level of Draevan's protectiveness. He kept her tucked to his chest, not letting an inch of space ride between them.

She asked if she should go ride her own horse, now that it was safer and they were far enough out of the kingdom, but Draevan's 'no' was so powerful that she didn't ask again.

At first she thought he was just afraid of their horses falling into the quicksand that surrounded the lands of the elven kingdom and wanted her to closely guide him. He seemed perturbed by the stuff, and she couldn't help but tease him by saying, 'You mean you never knew how the kingdom stayed so well hidden? Why people searching for it are never heard from again? Well, now you know what happened to them!'

He didn't have a sense of humor as dark as hers. Taric chuckled at the solved mystery. "Thank the gods they found *us* and we didn't have to go finding *them*!"

"They would have done anything for the shield," she replied. "Even if it meant keeping their word."

"If it meant so much to them, how'd they lose it to the giant?" Draevan's voice rumbled in her ear. She loved his deep, strong baritone.

"My great-great-great-great-great... probably add a few greats to that... grandfather was the king's twin brother... The king was born first technically, but my grandfather was smarter, and he wanted to grow the kingdom. There was a coop, and in the midst of it, he stole the medallion, which held a lot of the kingdom's power, and he disappeared with his wife and children, and a curse was put on all of his line. When the giant came down to the forest, years later, he was eaten by the giant, and the giant's had it since last month."

Taric snorted. "So the king had a hatred for your people because of some family upset that happened to his great-great-great..."

Her forehead wrinkled as she wondered if they were having a sort of communication problem. "No," she replied, shaking her head. "His *brother.*"

Draevan cleared his throat, and she felt the hand that was resting against her stomach tapping. "Honey, that probably happened nine hundred years ago," he drawled, as if he were a father telling his child that faeries didn't exist and wishing on a star didn't actually work. "It's not the same king."

She rolled her eyes to the side. "Of course it's the same king..."

"Kyra, the king would have to be nearly a millennium old," Taric educated with enthusiasm, as if aging was a concept she didn't understand. "Aside from how stupid he is for someone supposedly that age, no one's that old."

They didn't know. How they could not know, it was hard to say. Why would they want an elf-wife if they didn't want immortality? That's what all humans wanted! There was no other magic that would truly help them!

"We... Don't die... of old age..." she drawled. "You realize that, don't you? The only reason my line doesn't live that long is because it's hard living out here! Not to mention that we've been hunted down by the kingdom all that time. I don't think any untouchable, my kin, have lived past forty... But that's just because our ends have all been pretty horrible. The king, however, doesn't have anything around to kill him... Until you men came along."

She turned her head to look back and forth between them, even though they were hard to see in the low light of the torch Taric held up. She could see Taric and Draevan exchange censored glances, as if she'd just said something so crazy that they were worried about what to do with her.

"I'm serious!" Kyra exclaimed, throwing her hands up. "You have to believe me. That's why it was a big deal for the king to offer you any woman you wanted—because this," she brought up her wrists and showed them to her husbands, "brings you *immortality*. We become as *one blood*." She threw her arms up in the air when they still looked far less than convinced. "Why else would you marry one of us? If you just wanted sex, then you could have just taken me in the forest and had done with it! Why go through the hassle of marrying me?"

"Because," Taric replied slowly. He was hedging for a moment. He still obviously didn't believe what she was saying, but she was suddenly wondering what their other excuse was, "We want you to have our children."

She put her hand to her eyes. "Stop the horse," she said, putting her other hand on Draevan's thigh. She turned to look at Draevan and Taric again once the horse stopped walking. "I like both of you, very much," she said slowly, trying to press down her nervousness. "But as the king said—I cannot have your children. You're human and I'm elf kind. It's never been tried before, but it's likely to never happen."

"As you said before," Draevan said, patting her consolingly on the hip, "We are of one blood. We must be melded. You'll have our children, wife, just as soon as we get some on you."

Her forehead smoothed as the words, 'we must be' struck her. They both were very confident. "And what if I *can't* 'get your children on me'?" she asked, openly mocking the way Draevan put it.

Taric was quick to answer, his voice no-nonsense and firm, closing the argument. "Then we'll keep trying until you *can*."

She swallowed, feeling pressure. She hoped that it was just a game, breeding her. Much like it was a game to make her play the part of their slut while in bed… Because she would never have their children. It simply wasn't possible.

Not that they could be told that. They traversed the forest for a full two weeks, cutting straight through the heart of the Blue Forest to the Crystal Mountains, and wherever they found a safe plot of land they would stop to put down their bedrolls and at least one of them would take her.

The first night they had traveled until late noon the next day; she thought she wouldn't be taken just then because of how tired she and the men were. But apparently, weariness didn't matter. Draevan pulled her off her horse, and she was promptly pushed down on her hands and knees onto a thicket of grass afterwards. He pushed her down to the ground by her shoulders and then pulled her ass up into the air, rolling her skirts over her waist to bare her. He dipped two of his fingers into her folds and found that she was so wet that her juices were beginning to drip down her inner thighs. With no words or warning, he had pushed his whole length into her and immediately began to thrust his whole length in and out in very hard, nearly bruising thrusts.

She found that she loved it; every time his tight bullocks slapped against her they patted her clitoris until she was moaning and gritting her fingers into tendrils of grass before her outstretched arms. Somehow, in the wide-open, surrounded by all this nature, with only Taric standing by to witness and thumbing his own erection, it felt for a moment like they were both merely animals—ones who badly wanted to mate and get in touch with their own dark instincts. She screamed Draevan's name, sweating despite the cold air nipping on her skin, and came. Draevan hissed in a breath, and she felt him flow liquid heat deep into her, filling her full with pulse after never-ending pulse.

He caught his breath afterwards and slapped her on the bottom as he pulled out of her. "Keep that ass in the air," he told her firmly. "I don't want one *drop* of it to fall out of you."

She sighed, knowing why it was important. He wanted his seed to take. She languidly rolled her head over to see Taric, who gave her a sexy grin as he pulled his saddle from his horse. "Get that worried look off your face, elfling," Taric told her. "Your days of fretting are over. That's our job, now."

She smiled slightly and stretched, still knowing that wasn't even close to true.

* * *

The last month had been strangely pleasurable... In a strange and slightly perverted sense admittedly, but still, traveling back to the Northlands was more fun than traveling from there to the Blue Forest, and Taric had to blame Kyra for that.

She was uncannily clever about the endless stretch of Blue Forest, and now that they were to the base of the Crystal Mountains, she was even more helpful in navigating through the wood rather than on the dangerous roads through the valley. She said she had grown up at the foot of the Crystal Mountains, although she hadn't made back to her old haunts since her brothers were captured and killed there.

Instead of shedding weight as he and Draevan had on the way there in the middle of summer, they'd actually put on weight, and they were traveling in barren winter. Kyra knew where her kinsmen had hidden secret stores of food as well as the locations of hidden caves in which to rest. Not to mention she knew where all the small forest creatures and fish-swollen parts of the streams were.

Taric and Draevan figured that the Northlanders would nearly view her as a Goddess, especially the more barbaric villages dispersed in the mountains. She hadn't been educated like he and Draevan had been; she couldn't even as much as write her own name, but the villagers would highly respect the way she'd learned to harness nature.

And the girl was *insatiable*! It was hard to recall that she was a virgin when they'd married the girl. She didn't appreciate turn-taking—she wanted who she wanted when she wanted him, and she wouldn't be told no. Not that either man would say no—in fact, somewhere along the line, love-making had become an unspoken competition of skill between him and Draevan.

Their little elf-wife loved sex and sometimes wouldn't even let them rise in the mornings until she'd at least taken one of them into her mouth. She had begun to initiate the play now, and if she didn't come right out and ask for it, she would be as seductive as she could be, either bathing naked in the stream and wiggling her hips at them or bending over in a certain way, even sitting on their laps around the campfire to grind her bottom against their lengths... She could get them to come running, and if they didn't satisfy her as fast as she wanted it, she would openly and dramatically pout. Hell, if a day went by when she wasn't filled by one of them, she would stomp around and whine at them until she was bent over something and given a warming spanking or a firm fucking.

Taric didn't even mind the cold winter, because it made him to have to snuggle his naked body closer to his wife's...

Who was really muscular this morning...

Both men suddenly shot awake, realizing—seemingly at the same time—that they were not next to who they thought they were. To compensate, both rolled away to the opposite sides, climbing quickly out of the sleep roll. "What the fuck?" Taric accused.

Draevan looked like he was feeling just as violated. "Well, waking up to your ugly ass certainly does the job better than a cup of coffee!" he huffed angrily, immediately finding and tugging on his breeches. He looked around. "Where's Kyra?"

Taric looked around, then looked in the powder-covered ground around them. It was possible she was simply making water somewhere—but she knew better than to go off without telling one of them at least. They never let her just wander off alone. "Kyra!" he shouted into the quiet air around them.

His voice echoed, and when there was no answer, dread fell upon him like a heavy blanket. "Kyra!" he shouted again, louder. Again, nothing returned but the echo.

"Kyra!" Draevan shouted, tugging on his jacket over his newly-donned tunic. "Answer right now, or else we're tanning your hide for you!"

They stood still, making sure they didn't crunch a blade of frozen grass or rattle one leaf, listening for the sound of her voice.

Nothing.

Taric finished dressing quickly as Draevan grabbed his sword out of his saddle. "If she's alright, she's not sitting down for a while," Draevan grumbled angrily. He didn't fool Taric; Draevan was ripe with panic.

"She knows better than this," Taric said, finally pulling on his own sword sheath. "She knows that she has to keep in sight. She *knows*!" Despite the cold, he felt his face flush with heat, and that was before he tripped over her boots.

"Fuck!" he said, looking down and picking up one of the small riding boots Draevan hand packed for their journey. Kyra loved them; all except for when she was climbing trees... Which she did like she was a goddamned squirrel, and if she did walk on the ground, she would barely leave tracks. She was too light-boned, like a bird.

Draevan stood still, stunned. "Do you think she… *ran?*" Draevan asked, swallowing. "Or do you think the Dark Lord knows about her and—" Strangely, it nearly seemed that to Draevan, her running from them was more distasteful than if she'd been kidnapped. Taric found he felt the same way—Taric and Draevan loved her. Absolutely *loved* her. They never told her that—there was never a reason to say those words—but it had to have been clear to her. And they'd both thought she was actually beginning to have feelings for them as well.

Taric didn't want to hear it; once they started thinking up scenarios, they wouldn't be able to stop. He put up his hand to silence him, snapping, "Shut up, Draevan. Let's just go find her."

* * *

"Well hellooo, breakfast!" Kyra chirped merrily to the second pheasant she had ensnared in one of her brothers' old traps as she climbed down her tree. They had camped less than a mile from one of her family's old hunting grounds, where some of their old traps were still hidden and ready to be put to use.

She had just finished plucking the other three when she ensnared the fourth. She was becoming quite the huntress! The men had killed a deer the last week, but she was getting sick of deer jerky for breakfast, and she could tell Draevan, at least, was as well. He got grumpy when he was hungry, and even grumpier if he had food and didn't want to eat it… And damn it all, when he was grumpy, he didn't have his normal passionate desire to mate with her either. And that just wouldn't do! Nobody could work her nipples with his tongue like Draevan could. Having him over her was like having a large, comfortable blanket. He worshipped her body, sometimes taking her so slowly she wanted to cry. And when he took her fast, it was as if the

Earth was quaking. He'd pump into her so hard that she'd be walking bow-legged the next day.

Taric made love just as well but completely differently. He was more attentive, more watchful, every move was calculated... And he loved her bottom. He wouldn't take her there often, but he was always penetrating and teasing her with his fingers. She'd had orgasms so big from Taric's skilled digits that they'd left her ears ringing and her brain scrambling to recall what her name was, or what day of the week it was.

Yes, she liked her men. She liked how attentive they were, how sexy they were, and especially how they held her at night. They were definitely still brutes... But they had a tender side and definitely a funny side. They talked amongst themselves much less now, letting her into their private jokes and thoughts. They actually trusted her more now, and because of it, she was beginning to really trust them as well.

And she trusted them to wake up without her and spank her soundly if she didn't start wandering back to camp soon.

She cut the neck of the pheasant and grabbed its legs, hanging it upside down like the other one. She was quickly unplucking the bird when she heard the crunch of leaves behind her.

She turned and didn't see anything, but she didn't trust her eyes. Never had; she knew better. She was an elf, after all.

Her ear twitched slightly, tingling all the way down to her lobe.

She was being hunted. She could feel it, and if she listened close enough, she could hear breathing from maybe twenty or so paces away.

One... Two... Three... Four, Five...

Fuck.

They were trying to keep quiet, she knew, so she looked back at her pheasant and moved like she didn't notice the band of royal guards closing in around her. She'd been in this position not a month ago. She and her husbands had hoped that the guard wouldn't bother following them past the Blue-Crest River that they traversed two weeks before.

She tucked the pheasant neck on her belt as if she meant to go back to camp. That's when she heard a bow being rosined.

She waited for the 'pluck', and when it came she darted out of her position, scrambled left, and then scaled a tree faster than most could run upon the ground. She heard loud cracks and snaps as arrowheads fell around her, some bouncing clumsily from the tree. She stopped climbing as she felt one go into the bagginess of Taric's spare trousers she was wearing, which practically flowed around her legs. With a grimace, she tugged mightily and ripped the fabric with a yank of her foot upwards.

She glanced down and saw that that the five elf-men had come out of invisibility, their hard-lined faces squinting with disdain as they put a second set of arrows into their bows.

She went invisible and crouched down the long branch of a tree. She tugged off one of her pheasants and tossed it, hoping that it would make them think she hopped to another tree branch and dropped it.

The elves fell for it, their eyes going to where the naked pheasant fell and then lining the nearby tree rather than the one she was quietly crouched upon, holding onto the branch and taking quiet, small breaths.

She watched them, staying still and silent for over fifteen minutes as they tried to speculate over where she'd gone, saying that she had left because they would have 'heard her by now'.

Eventually, they left, heading towards the river, thank goodness, and not toward the camp, and she waited, listening carefully for about ten more minutes to make sure they were truly gone.

She climbed gingerly down the tree, her muscles aching and her legs cramped from crouching on the branch for so long. She picked up the pheasant that she had thrown earlier from the ground and dusted it off before walking tenderly back to camp.

It was three miles over terrain filled by old roots that came so far out of the ground that one had to climb around and through them. The terrain kept out larger animals, like deer, wolves, and bear, but it was a haven for smaller creatures and birds. She climbed up a root drawing against the side of a cliff near her camp where the ground was more clear and open for the sake of the horses, and as soon as her feet hit the ground, she scrambled up a tree after hearing a sound stomping through the forest.

She went invisible and scurried up the nearest tree, wondering if there was a bear or something—surely it couldn't have been her husbands, because they'd still be sleeping at this early hour...

Yet it was her husbands indeed! She exhaled a breath of relaxation, and her husbands saw her sitting on that branch in that moment, marked by Draevan non-too-happily announcing, "There she is!"

They hustled over to her, and she jumped down, eager to fill the space. All she wanted was their strong embraces around her, their protection, and to tell them everything that had happened that morning.

She collided with Taric, who had stepped out in front of Draevan, and he wrapped his hardened arms around her, tucking her close against his warm chest and then putting his hand to her hair as he kissed her forehead. Draevan came to the side of them and wrapped his arms around her as well. She was being squeezed tight for a long moment. "Gods, Kyra," Draevan sighed, kissing her temple and continuing to press his lips against her as he relaxed. "We thought something happened to you..."

He parted from her and looked very unhappily at the plucked quail, whose legs were tied to her belt strap. "You went *hunting?*" he accused, like she had done a great crime.

"My family had a hunting ground about three miles down in the valley," she said, her voice breathy as she pointed down the cliff. "There's game there year-round if you don't overuse it." She swallowed. Her throat was dry, and she didn't like the cold look in Draevan's eyes. He turned his back on her and walked to a nearby line of trees.

She looked up at Taric, who didn't look any more pleased with her. "We thought you'd run away. We were going to scour this forest for you, Kyra," he said, even though her mouth was open to begin talking about the Royal Guard on their heels. "Not to mention there are dangers in the woods, and there are people out to kill us!" He gave her a shake.

The shake rattled her whole body down to her toes, nearly giving her whiplash. "Think!"

"I know," she said, thinking he was talking about the Royal Guards. "And I saw—"

Taric reached down and unlashed her belt, his eyes intent and livid. "No!" In the next move, the quail, her dagger, and his pants fell down to the ground at her bare feet. There was nothing but that belt that hooked anything to her waist.

Even though he'd seen it all before, she covered her womanhood away from him as the cold air greeted areas she did not expect. "Taric, listen to me!" she cried, realizing that she was in hot water. "Down in the hunting grounds, I saw—"

Draevan grabbed her upper arm, and with a firm jerk, she skipped away from the clothing on the cold ground, feeling propelled to scramble forward.

Swiiish-swack! An ominous whistling rushed through the air.

Her eyes widened. "Ouch!" she screamed, high pitched and miserable, her brain struggling to process what was going on before another hot stripe of pain fell across her bottom once again.

"I *never*," Draevan gritted through his teeth as he brought a switch unpityingly down on her in a fury with hard, crisp stokes, "want you—to think—of disappearing— again! — You're too important—you're too smart for that—and I will bring your world—to—an—end if you defy us even *once more* on that!" She was busy trying to get out of his grip, trying to scream out for him to stop, but the words only coming out as unintelligible squeaks and shrieks. He didn't hold her firm enough to hurt her arm, and letting her run around him in a circle while he striped her bottom, her thighs, and even a few on her calves, seemed to suit him just fine.

When she tried to fall to her knees and cover himself, that's when he bent over and tucked her against his hip, letting her feet kick up from the ground.

His words hissed over her wails and her ridiculous cries for Taric to intercede. "You will always tell—us—where—you're—going—and you will never—EVER— go out on your own! — Do—you—understand—me?"

She clawed her fingers desperately into his trousers and his flank, trying to get him to let go of her.

SWACK! "Do you understand, Kyra?" he asked again.

She had to take a deep breath to cry out, "Yeees!" in a desperate wail.

He gave her ten more swipes without words, and the fire in her bottom felt like it had spread everywhere. She was sobbing like a baby before she was pulled off of his hip. He discarded the make-shift implement on the ground and let her go, spinning her up into another embrace.

She heard him sniffle.

Draevan? *Sniffling*? After he'd punished *her*? "I love you, I love you, I love you…" He whispered into her hair. "Don't scare me like that, okay? You're the most important thing in my life. And not just because of the prophecy. You're my goddess! I would die a million times over rather than let anything happen to you! Don't leave us. Don't ever leave us. If we lost you, we wouldn't know where to start looking!"

Prophecy? What prophecy? She had no idea what he could have been talking about. She wanted to ask, but she was dying to apologize. She didn't mean to scare Draevan this badly! Badly enough to make this big brute admit that he loved her—which he hadn't done before. She'd suspected it, she wanted to hear it, but the way he'd gushed it out was heartbreaking rather than heart*warming*.

Still, all that was coming out was tears and sobs. Her bottom throbbed and itched—she didn't even want to reach behind and rub it, afraid to irritate the skin even more.

Taric gently pull Kyra out of Draevan's arms and kissed her face. "We're not joking, Kyra," he said in stern, firm words. "You need to be safe. You can't go out on your own. Ever. Never ever. Do you hear?"

She nodded and sniffed, and he brought her into a soothing hug, shushing her in a lulling coo. "Let's bring her back to camp. Grab her clothes and those birds, will you?" he told Draevan, reaching down to sweep his arm under the back of her knees so that she fell into his arms. "You, missy, have a lot of explaining to do, you know. I'm also going to teach you to write, and I will not be nice about it. But for the gods' sakes, it would be nice to at least wake up to something that told us you were just out somewhere being naughty and breaking rules, not run away and not hurt somewhere in the middle of a forest I'd like to avoid for the rest of my life!"

Somehow, even through Taric's harsh words, the 'I love you', was just as clear as Draevan's whispers. She hugged her arms around him, feeling soothed for a moment even though his arm stretched uncomfortably across one of her angrier welts.

Suddenly she jumped, startled that she forgot about the guards even for a moment, and said, "There were royal guards in the forest down there where I was!"

Taric stopped walking, and Draevan, who was walking

next to him, froze and exchanged a dangerous expression with him.

Draevan looked down at her. "Did they see you?"

She nodded. "When I was hunting. I got away, but they can't be far behind."

Draevan took the sword out of his satchel and looked around. "They'll be invisible, won't they?" he asked dryly, even as he was looking for them. "Did they hurt you?"

"They ripped up my trousers a little, but I'm not hurt," she told them. "They're easy to fool, but they're not entirely stupid. They'll be able to track us, and if they came all the way out here, it means they're not stopping."

"Alright, here," Taric gently set her down on the ground. She pulled her tunic down her front, and Draevan passed over her trousers and her belt. She hissed a breath when she put them on—the linen felt like sandpaper. "We need to get back to camp in a hurry, honey," Taric said. He pulled out his sword, but his free hand found hers and grasped onto her tightly. "I'm sick of this shit," he seethed to Draevan. "Damn cowards with their bows, their stealth, and their stupid invisibility—how are we supposed to find them to kill them?"

Draevan growled, but after a moment he snorted. "We'll have to let them find *us*."

* * *

"Draevan," Taric sighed, dropping the tools he'd used to make up his booby-traps on the ground. "Are you eating the *bait*?"

"No," Draevan said, trying not to chew on the pheasant for a moment. It was hard to not to notice that the pheasant was missing a whole leg. After another second he growled, "I'm hungry!"

Taric rolled his eyes. "Eat the jerky."

Draevan set his jaw and gave him a crude gesture. "Eat *me*."

They were trying to produce smoke with a scent that would travel around the area where they knew the guards were already looking for them. Right now it was mostly burning, as was the plan—they needed the air sweet and smoky.

"My poor, starving husband." Kyra came along Taric's side, leaned down to where Draevan sat next to the fire, and kissed him. Afterwards, she smacked her lips, and then frowned at him. "Draevan, you taste like whiskey."

"I've watered it down enough, darling," he whispered to her. "I'm preparing the props here." Louder, he hooted, "I'm a man—I can have a drink when I want!" He gave a saucy nod of his head and a smirk. He reached out and tried to hook his arm around her waist to pull her onto his lap.

She stepped back from him. "No."

"Come sit," Draevan told her more plainly, patting his lap invitingly.

"I'm not sitting ever *again*!" she pouted, rubbing the bottoms of his old trousers she was still wearing and had journeyed in all the way to the Hidden Springs that day. According to her, it was the safest place to be to spring a trap on men who didn't want to be caught. The spring was part of a strange step, fed by a tall waterfall on the north of them and a leading to a long drop-off to the south. The west was blocked by the deep, still spring, and on the east was the only way for the elves to get in or out of their nook. Better yet, it was so overgrown with ivy and other foliage that a long-shot arrow wouldn't have a chance to make it to them.

Best of all, even Kyra's footprints were showing up in the loose soil under their feet. Even if they went invisible, they might still be able to see their attacker's location.

"I was only being *nice* by finding you food. I was going to be back before you woke up."

"Do us and yourself a favor," Taric said, "and don't do anything else *nice* for us. The true nice is waking up with you between us and *safe*, rather than waking up to a nightmare."

Taric had been lecturing her off-and-on for the better part of the day as they put booby traps together, so now she was looking at him with exasperation.

"Go take a dip while we pretend to get drunk. The hot water will feel warm against the welts," he advised, smiling kindly at her.

She pouted and closed her arms across her chest. "No. I'll just stand here. Besides, you don't want anyone else to see me naked, do you? They could be ambling up around us any minute!"

Taric shrugged. "They wouldn't live to tell about it," he replied.

She shook her head, stubborn, and stood there miserably. She was tired, and her hands drifted back to move across her well-spanked thighs.

Taric grumbled, grabbed some salve from his saddle bag, and went to sit down, pointing at his thigh.

She walked obediently to him but didn't seem to know what he had planned. "Pull down your trousers and bend over my lap," he said, and when her face distorted with dismay, he added, "Let's see what you made us do to you."

"That's not exactly how *I'd* put it," she sulked, but she carefully crawled over his lap.

He pulled her trousers the rest of the way down to her ankles. He whistled appreciatively, "Cousin—look at these."

Draevan leaned over to look. "I know," he agreed, running a finger over one of her welts, leaving her cringing. "I'm an artist."

Taric smirked, running the salve against one of her puffy welts. None had broken the skin, but they were still angry, swollen, and red. Prettily, he hadn't crisscrossed any of them, even if her position during the punishment had been less than ideal. There was a half-inch between each one on her bottom. "Well, Grandfather always did say you'd be good at *something*."

"Don't lather on that too thick," Draevan told him, pointing to the salve. "I don't want cause-and-consequence to get lost on this little huntress of ours."

"Just enough so she can ride a horse tomorrow without us getting smothered by her whining," Taric assured with a laugh.

"It's not like I whine often!" she whined.

Taric and Draevan smirked mischievously at each other.

"Whatever you say, wife," Draevan chuckled, then gave her a slap on her less-welted flank and got up to steal another drip of burnt meat off of the pheasant carcass.

Her fingers clenched against Taric's pants, "Ooowe!" she whined. "I have the meanest husbands in the universe…"

Taric chuckled to himself and carefully put his fingers into the salve and ran it along her welts. At first, she whined about how cold it was, and then she hissed at the pain when he paid attention to some of the most swollen of the welts. There was fewer on her thighs, and even less on her calves, but she squirmed and twitched as he put the soothing potion on her.

He was uncomfortably erect at the moment, and because of the way her squirms were becoming seductive wiggles, he knew that she knew it too. He smiled and cupped her sex with his hand. She emitted a cute, innocent little gasp, but she was wet.

"Is my little slut wanting something?" he rumbled coquettishly at her.

She moaned slightly, not answering, so he flicked her clit with his finger. He knew he had absolutely no time to salve up her welts, let alone to bed her right now. But he loved teasing her and getting her sexually frustrated, mostly because her pout was so cute and sexy.

"Tell me how much you want my cock, baby," he demanded quietly.

"Please, Sir... Fill me?" she replied, something that she had been taught to say—they were still working on getting her to talk filth in their ears.

Still, Taric had a sadistic side. He liked to tease her mercilessly. "Nope." Taric gave her a pat on the thigh and helped her up. "Now go feed and blanket the horses."

There was that pretty, gold-eyed pout that he'd grown to love. She pulled her trousers back on in a huff.

"If you're a good girl," he told her, "maybe we can have fun later. If not, I know another entrance that hasn't gotten any attention for a while."

She blushed and narrowed her eyes at him, knowing he was talking about her bottom. "There's something wrong with you, Taric," she declared.

Draevan laughed heartily, only to get interrupted by a 'ching-ching' sound of a small bell, announcing that the band of elves were close-by and that they were more than likely being watched.

It was show-time. If it worked on their wife, it would work on these higher-born elves too. They only had to act drunk.

Kyra had to play the part of the nervous-and-nagging wife who was constantly yammering about the dangers out in the woods, that they were being hunted by the king's men, that they should believe her... everything was said and done loudly, deliberately, trying to lull the spies into a false sense of security.

She played her part quite well, although she was sweating with nervousness. The drunker they acted, the more alone she acted. For a time, he wondered if she thought they were really truly drunk, possibly because Draevan helped himself to the most severely burnt part of the pheasant roasting on the fire.

Taric pretended to fall asleep first, resting upon a hidden shield. Draevan sat up, molesting Kyra openly as she whined and cried at his clumsy, handsy movements. He didn't last much longer.

After Kyra felt between them and snuggled up in the blankets, Taric and Draevan were more on high-alert than ever. They were made to wait—the guard only came in when the fire had burned down to embers, and they were invisible when they came in, their boots smacking the mud near the camp as they trudged through it, nowhere near as stealthy as Kyra could be.

Taric kissed the back of her neck. He hated this, truly. Draevan's idea was sound; he couldn't fear the king's guard on top of his future son's enemies as well. He had to do away with them and end it. But Kyra was helpless in a battle; she wasn't strong at all, and she weighed nothing—or seemed to; she was so elvish.

He would have to move fast. He squeezed Kyra's hand, just enough so that the approaching band wouldn't notice.

Taric heard a sword being unsheathed—one that did not belong to himself or to Draevan.

Draevan was the first to move, impatient for battle. He swung his body up, swinging with a sword he had hidden under a blanket. A gurgle came from the empty air of the night, and then an elven body became visible as it fell to the ground.

Taric struck out and hit another blade, and then he pushed Kyra back, out of the bedroll, and she pulled the shield up with her and ran behind the horses as if she was sure they'd protect her.

Though they had been the ones to defeat the giant, this battle was far stranger. They were fighting with footprints in the mud, using moonlight to see by. They had to fight by intuition, by listening, by imagining what might be running through the other's head. There were four of the elves left now, and they were fighting for their lives.

Draevan was quickly covering the way out, blocking them in the small sandbar.

That made the guards panic; he could hear their breaths speed up and their mumbling become desperate. They fought like small children, despite their astounding advantage, and in a dark moment of carnage and noise, swinging their swords, Draevan and Taric ended them like they were sheep at the slaughter.

They looked about, seeing bodies now, but no other footprints. "Killed two," Draevan panted.

"Yes," Taric nodded. "Me... too..." It settled upon them both at once that their count was off. Yet there was no one around them... "Kyra?" he called, swallowing.

Then one of the horses whinnied and stomped forward, exposing two shadows in the darkness, the vision clear. Kyra had a knife to her throat.

It was odd—the knife was at her throat, but Draevan and Taric were the ones having trouble breathing or swallowing. It felt like the knife was at theirs.

Taric felt horror akin to illness.

"Drop your weapons," the elf seethed, his pale yellow eyes looking demon-like in the moonlight.

Draevan and Taric couldn't have dropped their swords with any less hesitancy. "If you hurt her—if you put a scratch on her— by the gods, I will rip off your balls, shove them down your throat, and fuck you up the ass!" Draevan snapped angrily. His pulse could be heard in his tone, causing his voice to break every beat.

"I'm not going to get out of here without her—we know that. Just stay where you are and she might live a little longer," the elf hissed like a cornered animal. "Now move out of my way."

"What... where are you taking her? You can't just take her," Taric snapped. "We won't allow it. Let her go, and we will let you go."

The elf snorted. "She goes with me. We will let her go as soon as you turn yourself in to the king's mercy."

That was a bleak alternative; none of them would make it out alive that way...

Draevan swallowed and glanced helplessly at Taric. They weren't prepared for a hostage situation; neither of them had any idea what to do. They watched dumbly as the elf stepped forward, grasping their wife by the throat.

Kyra's eyes were wide as saucers, terrified.

"Keep moving, whore," the elf hissed at her, making sure to keep his eyes on Draevan and Taric the whole time. "Else they'll find you in pieces, or hanging from the highest tree where your kind belongs. Lord knows it dirties me just to touch you."

Kyra's eyes filled with pain and misery. Gods, Taric hated to see her pain. He knew her well enough now to know that all she wanted to do was gain the smallest measurement of acceptance and respect... Taric shuddered a breath, feeling worthless. There she was—led away helplessly while her husbands stood there like dickless—

They were at the tree line already. Draevan grabbed his sword. "I don't care what happens, he's not getting another fifty paces with her," Draevan swore between clenched teeth.

"Hyah!" There was a tightening, whip-like sound, and a shadow flew upside down from one of the trees.

Draevan and Taric raced over, watching Kyra pace around the flailing body, hanging by a noose tied around his heel, exactly like the trap they had ensnared Kyra with when they'd met. Kyra picked up the man's dagger from where it had dropped on the ground, coldly walking up to him. "It dirties me to touch you too," she told him, and slit his throat.

"Kyra, *gods!*" Draevan panted, slowing down and clamping his arms around her to drag her away from the hanging body. "You... You didn't have to—we would have killed him for you," he said, fretting. He eyed the noose. "I don't remember you making that booby-trap."

Their old response finally came back to them. "You weren't watching me closely enough." She shook her head, looking quiet and very, very tired. "I wanted him to know," she said quietly, "in case he was the last of my kind I will ever see... that I'm not untouchable." She looked up at them, looking like a warrior goddess in the moonlight. She was incredible. She straightened, her posture impeccable. "I'm a Giantsbane." She eyed the swinging body. "And I'm better than him. I'm better than them all."

With that, she dropped the dagger onto the ground and headed back to camp.

Draevan and Taric watched her as if spell-bound for a moment. Taric was the first to cut the silence. "Did you ever for a moment think that she might have not been mother of The One to Kill the Dark Wizard?" he asked him.

Draevan frowned. "I've doubted it before, yes. I thought, for a time, that there might one day be other giant-killers, and other elves... that the prophecy had nothing to do with us, or with her." He turned his head, and then patted his shoulder. "But I don't worry about that anymore. It's her, Taric. It's about her."

Taric smiled weakly, for the first time not skeptical of the prophecy. What a crazy life they had in front of them now. There was so much to do yet that it was nearly overwhelming... But for now, Taric could only nod and say weightily, "I know."

"We should tell her about... You know. The prophecy," Draevan told him. "Our village knows it. She's strong now—she can handle knowing."

Taric took a deep breath. "I don't want her to think that's the only reason we married her."

"That is the only reason we married her," Draevan replied strongly, then softened. "It's not the only reason we *love* her, and it's even not the only reason we take her into our bed. We're proud of her... We can't live without her." He frowned and shrugged weakly. "At least I couldn't. Could you?"

Taric sighed heavily. "No," he admitted. "I *couldn't* imagine it."

"Then the least we can do is tell her. Trust her."

Taric raised an eyebrow, smirking a little. "So you're

the one telling *me* to trust her now?"

Draevan agreed that it was odd. "I guess that's what they mean when men talk about women turning their world upside down, huh? Gods know, I barely know up from down anymore." He straightened. "To tell you the truth, I've gone sort of insane. I've even thought about killing you in your sleep."

Taric's eyes widened, but not with terror or even surprise. "I've thought about killing *you*!" he said, somehow relieved that he wasn't the only one who'd lost his mind since Kyra. "Just so I can have her to myself!"

"Exactly," Draevan nodded, but then smiled. "Our wife probably needs ten men just to keep her in line and keep her safe, yet she only has us two."

"That was also my conclusion," Taric admitted. He punched his cousin in his brawny shoulder. "So I guess I'll just have to deal with you."

"We'll have to learn to enjoy sharing." Draevan sighed and then waved his fingers around, adding, "That is, if she even speaks to us again after realizing that we've kept sort of... you know... Kept from her the fact that the Northern hemisphere depends on her."

Taric nodded and looked over at her, where she was kicking the river water with her toes as she sat on a boulder on the water's edge, dripping her legs over the side. "I'd rather fight the giant then tell her we've kept that from her for this long."

Draevan gave a wry laugh. "Me too, but unfortunately... We killed him already." Draevan gave him a shove in her direction and said, "Come on. Let's get this over with..."

CHAPTER SEVEN

Kyra pulled off her coat as she walked her horse inside the long tunnel within the Crystal Mountains. She hadn't spoken for five days, now, and she could tell her husbands were getting worried.

They were quiet now too, although they wasted no opportunity to coddle her. They'd even stopped at the dwarf village at the foot of the mountain, loaded up with supplies, and even bought her cake, hoping to get a smile out of her.

She had no smiles to give. Something about the weight of the world resting on her womb successfully getting fruited and her being able to raise some sort of ultimate warrior sort of put a halt on the ability to move her face that way. Her brain kept rotating it in her mind over and over and over… She didn't know how to use a fork for gods' sakes. How was she supposed to handle this sort of responsibility?

Hell, last week she didn't even think she could get pregnant by them. Now… There was a prophecy. The Northlands were known for their soothsayers… She might actually be able to bear children… It was technically very possible that she was pregnant already.

It didn't even matter if the prophecy was true. She was going to be going to a place where they very much believed it, and she would be watched and subjugated for the rest of her life... Or until the Dark Wizard was slain.

Draevan had begged for her to just 'be mad at them'. About what? If she was one of them, she wouldn't have told her either! And when they told her, she'd just taken a life for the first time! She was near tears, emotions broiling on the surface, still shaking from the sensation of having a blade under her throat.

The added news made her head feel like it was going to explode.

Now, she could still barely enjoy the Crystal Mountains... which she had never gotten to do before, because she'd never actually been in them... Walking through the caves of the Crystal Mountain was like walking around in a diamond. One lantern made the room as bright as day. The inside was also quite warm—a vast contrast to the outside.

"Let's camp here," Taric advised, pointing to a place along an inner-mountain stream as he jumped off his horse. "It's not like we have daylight to worry about. We should stop when we're ready, or else we'll be going all day and all night." He took her horse's bridal and led them both up to the stream before he put up his arms and helped her off.

Her husbands had been too weary of her anger, or emotions, that they hadn't taken her for days. She felt Taric's unrelenting erection through the fabric of his trousers when he helped her onto the ground, and her brain finally focused on it—on him—on the need inside of her.

She had gotten unused to going this long without one of them inside of her. She missed it. She just didn't know how to say that she wanted it, and that everything was okay, and that she forgave them for not telling her of the prophecy at all, and that she loved them.

She really, really did love them; it was impossible not to, especially now that she was used to their gruff words and ways in bed. She was used to threats of their firm-handed discipline, too. Once she'd gotten used to that, it was easy to see that they adored her, and she loved that they did.

She sighed, happy to be thinking about *them* for a change. Just them, and now, and not the future.

They glanced up as they built a fire just large enough to cook on and smiled hopefully at her, as if they were relieved to hear her make noise at all. Then, as if they were afraid of being rude by staring, they went back to their work. She closed her arms in front of her chest, chewing her lip, wondering how to start conversation after being silent for so many days. The silence was now beginning to feel awkward.

She walked around the nearest bend for just a moment, looking for something to do rather than hover over them, but as she heard them converse quietly with each other, seeming to be planning on 'who was going to try to talk to her' that day, she found herself pulling off the dress around her and letting it drop to the ground. She quickly braided her hair to pull it off the back of her neck, then straightened her shoulders and walked back out into the small cavern they had put the bedroll down in.

They looked at her, looked down, then seemed to realize she was naked and looked up, their eyes round, their muscles tense and glittering in the rainbow light within the cavern.

She put up her hand. "I don't want to talk about it," she said when Taric opened his mouth to say something. "I love you, and I trust you to decide what I do and don't need to hear. It's not like you don't have your own language, and I don't mind that. You would never say or do, or *not* say or *not* do, anything except if you thought it was for the best." She took a breath. "I want you."

Draevan was the first one to find his tongue. "Which

one of us?" he asked her.

She looked at them and blinked; she wasn't sure. She didn't want either one to just sit and wait his turn with her or to feel left out. "I'm not part of two families," she told him, gesturing to her marriage-markings on her wrist—she noticed long before that they were completely identical to each other. "We're all entwined; we're in the same family. I don't want you separately tonight. I want both of you, like I had you on our wedding night."

Taric swallowed and said, "So… You want us both at the same time?"

She controlled her smile. She could almost feel an excited energy filling up the air again. "I want to lose myself a little. I want you both however I can have you, and much and as hard as you can give me."

They were very still, and very thoughtful, just blinking excitedly at her like children about to receive a present. She couldn't help but break into a laugh. "Well, if neither if you want me, I'll just take care of myself…" she threatened, turning her hip.

She didn't even get a foot entirely off the ground to step forward when she felt spun around and tilted over Draevan's broad shoulder. She squeaked with excitement as Draevan exclaimed, "If we're dreaming, I don't want to wake up. Did you hear what our wife just demanded, Taric?"

"I did. And I won't disappoint. Tonight, we'll hump any residual silence right out of her!" He gave a laugh. "Put her down, you ass… I've been thinking of this pussy of hers like a man lost in the desert dreams of water!"

Draevan dropped her to her feet on the bedrolls, and Taric, who had apparently been in a rush to get nude, brought her down to lie on the mat. His eyes were so intense that she found herself embarrassed by his touches. He nipped at her breasts and the skin on her belly until her bottom was all the way on the padding; then he grabbed her thighs and with a yank and an "oof!" she found herself on the flat of her back with her thighs up in the air, presenting her dripping cunny to him.

He finished spreading her legs apart and pressed his middle and index finger deep into her until his knuckles hit against her clit. She bit her lip, watching the seductive, animalistic look on his face as he plunged his fingers deep into her. "You're soaked," he told her, which was surely obvious before they started; he just liked to say it to make her cheeks blush. "Does this feel good, my little elfling?"

She nodded, still chewing on her bottom lip timidly.

"Use your words, darling," he told her. "I missed the sound of that sexy voice of yours. Do you like having something inside of you?" he inserted a third finger.

"Yes," she hummed, thrusting her bottom up to meet his hand's thrusts.

"Good, my slutty little wife, because you are going to be full this evening. We are going to use your three sexy little holes how we see fit," he gave her one of those cat-who-caught the cream grins.

That made her a little nervous. She wasn't used to taking him up her bottom yet; it had only happened a few times, and she could never truly relax enough to make it feel as good as he promised it could be. "That's right, baby," Draevan said, flattening himself next to her. He was naked now as well, and the head of his rod was thick enough that it nearly reached his navel, peaking far above the mess of blonde hair at its base. "Daddy's going to take this tight little bottom for himself, especially after hearing so much about it."

She had a very bad feeling that he was 'Daddy' now. She actually liked when they called themselves that—there was something some dominant about it, mixed with just the right bit of 'naughty'... That being said, Draevan was even bigger than Taric. "Not my bottom," she begged Draevan. "Even Taric's too hard, I—"

"Shh, shh," Draevan said, then sucked one of her swollen nipples into his mouth. "It will feel good," he promised. "Just trust me, baby."

She whimpered and would have maybe argued more, but Taric pressed his tongue at that moment onto her swollen nub, and she gasped out wildly, bucking her hips up again. "Gods, you're excitable!" Taric laughed. "Don't rush this, little one. We've got all night."

She felt a surge of impatience flash through her body. Once she got 'in the mood', her men told her she had no patience. She wanted to cum right away; she was certain they could make it happen for her in a single minute, but sometimes they'd stretch it out for hours before letting her have her release.

But they liked making this an event, and she couldn't blame them for that; every time they made her suffer with waiting, she felt closer to them, more satisfied afterwards.

"Draevan," she whined as he nipped her nipple more. "That feels so good…"

"Don't stop, Cousin," Taric suggested and grabbed her arms. "Just pause. I'm taking her, here…" He lay down on his back, and Draevan's mouth left her just as he and Taric arranged her entrance above Taric's cock, then slowly lowered her body. She moaned, pleasure saturating her as she took in Taric's length.

Draevan returned to her nipple, pawing the other wildly as Taric grabbed her bottom with both hands and forced her weight up and down in rapid succession, slamming his length into her, deep. Her back arched back, her eyes fluttering.

"Alright, I can't take this," Draevan announced, his voice hardened with lust. He got up on his hands and knees and crouched over her, feeding her his length into her mouth. "Come on, honey…" he cooed as she lovingly lapped him with her tongue and took him in. "That's my girl. Gods, you know how to suck a cock, elfling. I won't even tell anyone how good you do this," he grumbled. "I don't want anyone trying to steal you away, and they would, because your mouth is… gods… so good…"

He took her braid gruffly with his hand and began to control his thrusts into her mouth, the head of his phallus touching her throat with every move. According to Draevan's expression, he wasn't lying—he was in heaven. His eyes were nearly completely black, looking drunk and at the same time possessive of that part of her body.

At the same time, Taric was pressing into her pussy, his length hitting her cervix. Just as she was certain she'd feel him spray his juices into her, he pulled out. "I want a piece of her ass first," he declared. "I'll get her ready for you."

As graceful as dancers, the men moved in their positions. She was crying like a kicked puppy about losing Taric's warm cock form her wanting pussy. "Don't worry, honey," Taric said, pushing her forward onto her knees. "It won't be empty for long. Get that bottom up." He gave her bottom cheek a loud, echoing slap with his command.

With a disappointed 'harrumph', she complied. "You're going to hurt! Can't you just have your way with my cunny?" she asked in a pout.

Taric cupped her sex and rubbed some of her own juices up to her bottom hole to lubricate her. "You know what good husbands do with pouty wives?" Taric teased, although his tone was gruff as he rubbed his cock against her small hole. "They stuff their bottoms full of cock..."

She froze, intimidated by the idea. "Taric!" She felt a delightful penetration as he slipped a single finger in and pumped it in and out a few times before pressing the smooth, hard head of his cock into her. She winced, but then Draevan was suddenly right there, holding up her head, and kissing her. "Relax," he soothed, brushing her hair. She couldn't help it; there was something about Draevan's deep voice that eased her muscles. "That's a good girl... I know it's hard, but just take in a deep breath and let it out..."

Taric's penis pressed through her tight rectum, stretching her opening. She sucked in air, and so did he. "She's so tight..." Taric hissed, and pulled out of her for a second before pushing himself back in, this time going deeper. He repeated the process.

"It hurts," she whined, looking up at Draevan.

He kissed the top of her pointing ear. "He'll make it feel good. Taric, give her a moment."

At his command, Taric buried his length fully into her and stilled. She whimpered slightly for a moment, but eventually she took a deep breath and didn't feel any pain anymore.

"That's it, baby. Relax that bottom. Feels better, doesn't it?" Draevan cooed, stroking some strands out of her face. He looked over her head and asked, "And what's wrong with *you*?"

She looked over her shoulder and saw that Taric had a tensed, pained look on his face. "Trying not to come," he responded. "Fuck, it's tight." He gave a short laugh and then started thrusting.

Oh, my... She was beginning to perspire, her whole body feeling hot and warm. Her body hummed at Taric's intensity as he began to pump into her harder. "Draevan," she said, looking at him hungrily. "I want you in my mouth, *now*."

"Woah," Draevan said, looking taken aback by such a snarling order. He smirked. "Don't say I don't spoil you," he joked. He put a knee up and to the side, giving her better access to his cock, which he was pumping with his hand until she put her lips around it. He stroked his hand down her neck and back, petting her like she was a cat.

She felt a bead of sweat drop against her bottom. Taric was gripping her thighs tightly in his fingers, thrusting viciously now. "You like that, don't you?" he asked. "Being filled in two holes?"

She flushed again, feeling naughtier than ever. "Mmmhmm," she agreed flirtatiously with her lips still suckling the head of Draevan's thick manhood.

"Of course you do, you little slut," Taric said, giving her bottom another firm slap. "Draevan—she's got a warm cunt here that needs filling."

"If she likes being filled in two holes, let's see if she likes being fucked in two," Draevan replied mischievously. They hadn't ganged up on her since her wedding night, but somehow them talking to each other was sexy to her—she had both of her husbands' attention at the same time, and they were working together to bring her what she was already sure would be an orgasm she'd never forget.

Taric pulled out for a moment, and Draevan lay down and slid her up along his chest, spread her legs wide to each side of him, and kissed her deeply as he guided his cock into her.

She thrust wildly against him in return to his own movements, groaning at how his thickness felt in her.

She thought Taric would come along to her front, but he didn't. Instead, he came and squatted behind her and lined his hard rod back against her swollen anus. She gasped, but before she realized what he'd planned, Draevan froze and Taric pushed himself inside of her, panting.

"You start," Taric wheezed, sounding like he had his cock in a vise.

Draevan chuckled and began to thrust inside of her again.

The sensation was incredible—she felt so stretched, so full, so overwhelmed with pleasure and pain. Taric started pumping in and out of her ass, as well. One after another, one would be thrusting up while the other thrust back, working in perfect rhythm.

She was screaming, but she didn't know why. It felt like she was going to burst with lust; she could feel the orgasm begin to grow to the point that she was going to start sobbing soon if they didn't let her come; she could feel her throat begin to restrict as tears stung her eyes.

"Are you gonna come on your daddies' cocks, honey?" Draevan asked her, filling her brain with naughtiness.

The words were like Draevan pushed a button. "Fuck!"

she cried. Taric put an arm around her, and they all jerked, roared, and groaned at the same time. She could feel their cum spurt, their last hungry thrusts continue languidly, and her muscles milking them dry.

They stayed still, panting for a long time.

She thought she was done, until Taric started to move within her again. He actually felt hard already...

"I'm not fucking *done*." Taric swallowed dryly and continued. "I want to blow into that pussy, too. Let's fill her until it's dripping down her thighs."

"Taric, you're so *vulgar*!" she found herself chiding over her shallow breaths. "Where did you hear such words?"

"Whorehouses," Draevan answered with a soft chuckle, and then looked over his shoulder. "I want in her ass. This will work well." He groaned and sat up, pulling himself completely out of position.

She blinked, scrambling for words, but they were already picking her up and manipulating her body. Both pulled out of her, leaving her feeling strangely chilly in the hot room. But then Draevan turned her gently, put his arms under her arms, pressed her back to his chest, and leaned backwards onto the ground, grabbing her knees and spreading them wide apart. He relaxed his arms merely to match his cock up to her anus. "You're too thick, Draevan!" she complained. "You're gonna hurt me!"

"Oh, my poor sweetheart," he hummed in her ear, biting her earlobe. "You always say that before you're begging for more." With that, he gave a firm thrust into her.

For a second, tears spilled down her face at the burning pain, but just as Taric had done earlier, he waited, and eventually began to hump her from behind, thrusting his arms up and down. It was as if her weight was nothing!

Thank the gods she married two men and not any elves... Not that she was offered marriage by her own kind, but she was certain that sex would never have felt so powerful. Her kind weren't nearly this strong.

Taric kneaded his cock in his hand and knelt between their spread legs. "The most fucking beautiful pussy in the world," Taric groaned as he eased himself into her. She moaned and let Taric press his face against her breasts as he thrust, nibbling and kissing her in his own skillful way.

"I'm going to cum so deep into you..." Taric promised her, then nuzzled her breast and nipple. "Are you happy you wanted both of us at the same time, baby?" He pulled all the way out and then thrust hard all the way back in so that her breasts bounced from the impact.

"Oh, gods, yes!" she gasped. She was in heaven. She had no idea why she was crying, but tears rolled down her cheeks. "Gods, you both feel so good..."

"And there's plenty more where that came from, honey," Draevan groaned under her. "You're our dream woman... And we don't ever plan to wake up."

"We won't ever have to," Taric assured. "Our sexy slut, our beautiful wife... Reason for living..."

She closed her eyes, wondering if it was possible to be any more loved or in love than she was right then. If anybody had told her a few months ago that there were feelings like this, she would have called them insane.

Thank the Gods for prophesies, Giants, and her life as she knew it. She was certain she wouldn't change anything that could have veered her from the path she was on right that moment.

Now, she was happy about moving forward... With her sexy, wonderful, protective humans. Her husbands, now and for always.

CHAPTER EIGHT

Draevan grinned when he heard Kyra's flute from across the road before he even opened up the gate to his home. He remembered it being annoying and ghostly when he'd first met Kyra in the forest, but now it was a comforting sound... a sound that cried 'home.'

"Hey, hey now!" Draevan came through the front gate of his brick manor house, where the courtyard garden was already in full bloom. The village children had found their way in there again, probably magnetized there by the flute-playing, and were all either dancing about or begging to touch his wife's hair, as if they would die if they couldn't.

Three children not even knee-high were rubbing their rosy little cheeks against the soft, white strands. Before she'd come, no one had ever seen an elf before, nor any young woman with white hair. "Go on, now. What did I say? She doesn't need your sticky fingers all over her hair, you little miscreants!" he chided adoringly. Somehow, he liked the look of his extremely pregnant wife surrounded by fifteen school-aged children and hundreds of flowers. His mind simply couldn't produce a more peaceful image.

That being said, he still wanted to annoy his wife in peace and quiet. "Go on, now," he told them. "Go home, or else I'll get out a switch!"

The children scooted around the garden, giggling. He frowned. He was one of the fiercest warriors currently alive, yet the village children all thought he was a giant pushover.

"Where's Taric?" he asked. One of them always needed to be home to be with Kyra... since one of them always seemed to be called away. The king of the North had declared them as the lords of their entire province. They were honored at first, and then realized that they had been snookered—they had hoped to lounge around all day with their wife for a while with all their gold! Instead, like fools, they accepted the hardest-job imaginable: governing.

She smiled softly at him, contentment spilling forth from her golden eyes. "He's walking the midwife back to her home. He'll be back any moment."

Draevan's brow crinkled. "Why? What's wrong?" He put a hand around her extremely swollen stomach. For such a small frame, her belly was so huge she could barely get out of her chair without help.

"You know why. You and Taric are so nervous about this pregnancy that you come near to a heart-attack if I have indigestion. I told him to get a healer for himself, and he left and came back with a midwife!" she nagged.

He gave her a chiding glance. "There's nothing funny about our worry, I assure you. We just want everything to go off without a hitch. Did you think the baby was due?" he asked her.

She shook her head and smiled at him. "Taric did, but there was no pain. Just so much movement, I thought a ballet was being put on in there..."

Suddenly, Taric's hands appeared on the side of the fence, and he bounded over it, jumping over to the other side, looking completely out of breath as if he'd run the mile back as fast as he could. "Kyra..." he panted, putting his hands on his knees.

"You could have walked to the door," she chided,

pointing to the garden's entrance.

"The midwife wouldn't tell me *anything*!" he huffed angrily. "What happened? What did she say?" Taric asked her firmly. "When did she think the baby was coming? Tomorrow? Next week?" he asked hopefully.

She laughed and shook her head. "No, much later than we thought."

"Why?" Draevan asked, incredulous. "How could that even be! Have you seen you lately? When we used to joke about getting you so pregnant you'd fall forwards, we meant it as a joke, but that's where you're headed!"

"Well, you got me overly with-child, it seems, so don't take that tone with me. It's not my fault. You'll have to bear another two months with a wife the size of a house." She rubbed her hand across the silk of her dress above her belly.

Taric and Draevan re-processed her words. "What do you mean?" Taric finally asked; he claimed to be the smarter one of the two of them and had yet to figure it out.

She tried to purse her lips, her seriousness completely non-existent. "I mean you gave me *two* little warriors to chase after, not just one, and they're already giving me trouble."

Taric dropped to his knees, looking like he was indeed going to hyperventilate for a moment. In the next, he crawled over to her, put his face to her belly, and kissed it.

Draevan was quickly busy kissing the source. "Two!" he said, pulling back just to exclaim it to the sky, and then he kissed her again.

Bursting with excitement, both men shot to their feet and embraced each other. After a moment, they realized they hadn't hugged since they were small children and pulled apart, settling for a handshake.

"Uh, well-done," Taric said, rubbing his hand on his neck.

Draevan smiled wider than he ever had before; his face

was already hurting. "Same to you, Cousin. Good work."

"Of course, I need no congratulations," she huffed.

"I would congratulate you, wife," Draevan told her. "But if you thought we were insane before… You're about to see us in a whole new light."

"Uh, having two ridiculous husbands is hard work," she groaned, rolling her eyes. When they were done rolling though, those beautiful gold specks twinkled at them. "But I wouldn't have it any other way."

THE END

ABOUT THE AUTHOR

Since the early age of three, Korey Mae Johnson has had an interest in spanking, which as the fascination grew through time, caused her to be an erotic spanking novelist.

All of her creative juices are squeezed from her real-life. She and her husband, James, is in a domestic discipline relationship and he is her muse… A very strict muse who's always handy with a paddle or a threat!

She doesn't like to sit on one genre for very long—she has it in mind to write a diverse collection of stories, from love-torn sheriffs to fated-mate aliens to handsy goblins to grumpy wizards, and she's always looking for what's going to be next!

After residing in Austin, TX for the last five years, they have recently moved to Albuquerque, NM and have two cats—neither of whom appreciate deadlines.

Check out her website at
http://koreymaejohnson.stormynightpublications.com
Or follow her on Twitter @KoreyMaeJohnson

STORMY NIGHT PUBLICATIONS WOULD LIKE TO THANK YOU FOR YOUR INTEREST IN OUR BOOKS.

If you liked this book (or even if you didn't), we would really appreciate you leaving a review on the site where you purchased it. Reviews provide useful feedback for us and our authors, and this feedback (both positive comments and constructive criticism) allows us to work even harder to make sure we provide the content our customers want to read. Reviewing stories you enjoyed also helps them sell better, which in turn leads to more high-quality work from your favourite authors in the future.

Adding keywords and tags (on Amazon, Barnes and Noble, etc.) really helps as well!

If you would like to check out more books from Stormy Night Publications, if you want to learn more about our company, or if you would like to join our mailing list, please visit our website at:

http://www.stormynightpublications.com

Printed in Great Britain
by Amazon